A wave of relief washed over him, and a feeling he barely recognized and dared not name was left on the shore of his heart.

Summer's eyes widened in recognition, and for just a second Theron thought he might have seen something like hope spark in her eyes.

As if tethered to her, he approached with one step. And then another. And another until somehow he was within an inch of her and his hands were reaching to frame her face and his mouth was claiming hers and he felt as if he was *home*.

He'd been lying to himself for months—he hadn't put her out of his mind. He'd kept her there, the memories of her locked away, and the moment that he'd seen her again they were all unleashed. This was what he'd needed, just so he could breathe, he thought as he pulled her flush against his body and...stopped.

He opened his eyes to find hers staring at him, shock and something horrifyingly like fear sparking to life in them. He pulled back and reached out at the same time, his hand unerringly finding the curve not of her stomach but a bump. Just about the right size for a...

The Diamond Inheritance

A map that leads...to forever?

When Skye, Star and Summer find out their
mother is gravely ill, they know they have to act—
quick! Yet the announcement at their estranged
grandfather's funeral of a windfall for the Soames
sisters could be the answer to all their prayers.
Only, to secure the fortune, they *must* track
down the Soames family diamonds. And their
unexpected treasure trail will bring each of them
into close quarters with a dangerously irresistible
billionaire...

Grab your passport and escape with...

Benoit and Skye's story
Terms of Their Costa Rican Temptation

Star and Khalif's story in
From One Night to Desert Queen

Summer and Theron's story in
The Greek Secret She Carries

All available now!

Pippa Roscoe

———

THE GREEK SECRET SHE CARRIES

HARLEQUIN
PRESENTS

PRESENTS

PLEASE RECYCLE
THIS PRODUCT IS RECYCLABLE

Recycling programs
for this product may
not exist in your area.

ISBN-13: 978-1-335-56819-9

The Greek Secret She Carries

Copyright © 2021 by Pippa Roscoe

This edition published by arrangement with Harlequin Books S.A.

For questions and comments about the quality of this book,
please contact us at CustomerService@Harlequin.com.

Harlequin Enterprises ULC
22 Adelaide St. West, 40th Floor
Toronto, Ontario M5H 4E3, Canada
www.Harlequin.com

Printed in U.S.A.

Pippa Roscoe lives in Norfolk near her family and makes daily promises to herself that this is the day she'll leave the computer to take a long walk in the countryside. She can't remember a time when she wasn't dreaming about handsome heroes and innocent heroines. Totally her mother's fault, of course—she gave Pippa her first romance to read at the age of seven! She is inconceivably happy that she gets to share those daydreams with you all. Follow her on Twitter, @pipparoscoe.

Books by Pippa Roscoe

Harlequin Presents

Virgin Princess's Marriage Debt
Demanding His Billion-Dollar Heir
Rumors Behind the Greek's Wedding
Playing the Billionaire's Game

Once Upon a Temptation

Taming the Big Bad Billionaire

The Diamond Inheritance

Terms of Their Costa Rican Temptation
From One Night to Desert Queen

Visit the Author Profile page
at Harlequin.com for more titles.

This book is for my sister, Kate.

I would not be where I am without her,

I would not be who I am without her.

Love,

always,

Xx

PROLOGUE

Last night...

THERON THIAKOS STALKED the damp London street, cursing the rain. It just never stopped. How could people live like this? he angrily asked himself, longing for the piercing heat and pure bright sun of Greece, the glittering blue sea that sparkled enough to make a person squint. The cloud-covered night gave the Mayfair street an air of mystery as he came to stand before the impossibly exclusive private members club, Victoriana.

Before him, two men stood either side of a door with such thick black gloss the paint looked like running water. The Tuscan columns supporting the portico spoke of riches and a sense of history that struck a nerve. Theron bit back a curse. This was exactly the kind of superior, expensive establishment that would appeal to Lykos's ego. Theron made to step forward when, shockingly, one of the men raised his hand to stop him.

'I'm here to see Lykos Livas,' Theron stated, not

bothering to conceal the distaste in his tone. He had neither the time nor the patience for this. The anger in him was overpowering and he wanted someone to blame. *Needed* someone to blame. And he knew just the person.

The other doorman nodded, holding the door open and gesturing Theron towards a woman wearing some sort of strange green tweed trousers that cut off at the knee and a waistcoat. Lykos had always had a flair for the dramatic, but this was so… English. *Old* English.

The immediate press of warmth that greeted him after the cold London night was a blessed relief. His mouth watered at the thought of the whisky he'd fantasised about for the entire drive down from the Soames estate in Norfolk where he'd left Summer standing on the stone steps, unable to face the look in her eyes as he drove away.

He'd lost everything. Absolutely everything.

Theron followed the hostess weaving her way through a surprisingly large establishment, completely decked out—as one would imagine—in furniture and furnishings from the Victorian period. And, despite the negative bent of his thoughts, he couldn't help but be impressed by the bar that stretched the entire length of the main room. Two houses, at least, must have been knocked together to create such a space.

He caught sight of his quarry, sitting at a booth of deep green leather with a woman no less exquisite than to be expected in Lykos Livas's company. Theron's gaze barely touched the brunette, his mind instead seeing rich golden hair, hazel eyes and lips that were ruby-red when full of desire and pale when devastated.

His fingers pulsed within his fist as Lykos finally turned to acknowledge him.

'This is all your fault,' Theron charged, his tone firm and bitter.

Lykos stared at him for a moment, his gaze so level Theron wondered if he'd even heard the accusation. Then he blinked that silvery gaze. 'I'd say it's good to see you but—'

'We are well beyond niceties, Lykos, so I'll say again, this is all your fault.'

'That depends on what "this" is,' Lykos said over the rim of his glass before taking a mouthful of his drink.

Inhaling a curse, Theron turned to the brunette. 'Leave us.' He hated being so cruel but he was at his wits' end.

'That is hardly necessary,' Lykos protested half-heartedly.

'It's not as if you won't find someone else to play with,' Theron said truthfully, turning his back on the girl as he looked for the hostess. 'Whisky?' She nodded and disappeared into the bar's darkness.

'True,' Lykos replied with a shoulder shrug, watching his companion leave in a huff before narrowing his eyes at Theron. 'I see you once in ten years and now you won't leave me alone?'

It was a relief to speak in his native tongue again. It had been—what?—a week since he'd left Athens and found himself in that hellhole in Norfolk. Some found the Greek language harsh, but to Theron it flowed like *tsipouro* from Volos and tasted like honey in *loukoumades*.

'This is not the time for jokes, Lykos.'

'You never did have a good sense of humour,' he groused.

Theron's drink arrived and he slipped into the now empty seat. He palmed the glass, staring at it as if he hadn't spent the last three hours wanting it.

'You'd best bring the bottle, *glykiá mou*,' Lykos said, leaning well into the server's personal space. Not that she seemed to mind. At all.

'What are you doing in London anyway?' Theron asked before challenging himself to only take a sip of the liquid he wanted to drown in.

'I like it here.'

'I don't believe you. I don't believe that any Greek worth their salt would enjoy all the…*grey*,' Theron said with such distaste it was as if the colour had taken up residence on his tongue.

'Grey? I'm not quite sure I've seen London during the daytime hours. Is it that bad?' Lykos asked, appearing to sincerely ponder it.

'Yes. But Norfolk is worse.'

Lykos's silver eyes narrowed and Theron's dark gaze held the challenge. 'Is that so?' Lykos asked.

'It is. They've even named a paint after it.'

'What, Norfolk?'

'Yes. It's grey.'

Lykos sniggered into his glass, before sobering and then sighing. 'What did you do?'

Theron clenched his jaw at the accusation. For just a moment it had been like it had always been between them. The banter flowing freely from the bone-deep knowledge of each other. But that was before Lykos had walked away from their friendship.

'If you're looking for absolution,' Lykos warned, 'you've come to the wrong damn place,' he went on before eyeing up the bottle of Glenglassaugh the waitress had placed on the table as if he wasn't sure he wanted to waste such good alcohol on Theron.

Theron shook his head, frustrated with the man who'd once been like a brother to him. 'I don't need absolution. I need to know why you called me a week ago.' Theron knew with absolute certainty that he was involved in all this somehow, but he needed to hear it from Lykos.

'To taunt you, of course,' Lykos said with a smile that had more than likely charmed women right out of their underwear. 'When your holiday fling turns up at my door—'

'Watch your mouth,' Theron growled.

'Ooh, touchy.' Watching Theron from the corner of his eye, Lykos continued. 'When the lovely Ms Soames arrived at my door trying to offload a fifteen-million-pound estate in the country for a third of the market value, I just wanted to brag. I've always wanted a castle.'

'It's not a castle.'

'Oh?'

'And it's rundown. There are holes in the walls and it's freezing. All the time. And the damp...' Theron threw his hands in the air as if in despair.

'Oh, well, that wasn't in the sales pitch. Is that why you're here? To talk me out of buying the estate?'

Theron thought about it for a moment too long. 'Buy the estate,' he said tiredly. 'And it's worth the market value, Lykos. Don't take advantage of a vulnerable woman.'

Lykos slammed his glass down on the table, ignoring the stares it drew from the other guests, his eyes shards of ice but the burn in them white-hot. 'There's a line, Theron, and you are skating dangerously close to it.'

Theron wanted to bite back, wanted the anger Lykos threatened. His pulse pounded and he welcomed it, his breath audible now as his lungs worked hard. They stared at each other, while Theron waged an internal war and Lykos waited to see what he would do.

Gritting his teeth, Theron decided it was better to leave than to cause a scene and got to his feet.

'Oh, sit down before you break down,' Lykos bit out.

Theron stared at the doorway long enough to realise that he didn't have anywhere else to go.

'Break down?' he asked.

'I can practically feel the tears from here. Drink that,' Lykos said, passing him a large measure of whisky, 'before you start weeping all over the place. *Then* have the kindness to leave before you scare off the rest of tonight's entertainment.'

'You're a real piece of work, you know that?'

'Theron, as hard as this is to believe, I really don't care what got your knickers in a twist.'

'You would have once.'

'And you chose Kyros,' Lykos growled.

'No,' Theron shot back. '*You* left.'

'And you could have come.'

'And how would that have repaid the man who gave us *everything*?' Theron demanded.

'That was always your problem. What could ever be equal compensation for what he did for us? What could you give him that would repay such a thing?'

Theron turned away from the demand in his oldest friend's gaze and stared into the whisky, trying to ignore the feeling that he might have finally found something worthy of such a debt.

His heart.

And his child.

'Fine,' huffed Lykos. 'You may explain, if it will take that look off your face.'

Summer paced before the fire in the Little Library. Back and forth, back and forth as her eyes went from wet to dry, red to pale. But her heart ached as if she'd never stopped crying.

This room had become her sanctuary in the last two months, every inch of it as familiar to her as if she'd lived here all her life. But instead of seeing books that would make the British Library jealous, she saw eyes, dark like coals, making her shiver from the heat. Eyes that had laid her bare, exposed her soul. Her heart pulsed and her core throbbed as if taunting her, reminding her of the night before, as he'd thrust into her so deep and so deliciously she *still* ached from the pleasure. She turned and paced back past the fireplace where flames danced joyously as if there was nothing wrong, as if her world hadn't just shattered into a million pieces.

She brushed her hair back from her face. Six months ago she had been a naïve third-year geophysics student whose only worry was how to pay her sisters back for working all hours to pay for her to go to university. And now?

She was pregnant.

And yet she couldn't afford to think about it. She couldn't think about Theron Thiakos or even her father, Kyros. Now she *had* to think about her mother and sisters. About finishing the treasure hunt she, Star and Skye had been sent on by the grandfather they'd never met. The task? To find the Soames diamonds, hidden over one hundred and fifty years ago by their great-great-great-grandmother from her abusive husband. Clues had been found, coded messages translated, and her sisters had travelled the world to track down the elements needed to find the jewels.

It had been easy to hide her baby bump three weeks ago, when Skye had flown first to Costa Rica and then to France to locate the map of secret passageways that led throughout the Norfolk estate. And Star had been so full of romance when she had left for Duratra in the Middle East, searching for the one-of-a-kind key made by joining two separate necklaces that her sister had missed all signs of Summer's pregnancy too.

Meeting the terms of the will, she had been forced to stay behind. She had scoured their great-great-great-grandmother's journals, searching for clues about exactly *where* Catherine had hidden her family's jewels, but hadn't been able to find any. But if they did find the jewels, the sisters would have met the terms of their inheritance and be able to sell the estate in order to pay for their mother's lifesaving medical treatment. That was *all* that mattered right now. The jewels. Her mother's health. She couldn't think of anything else.

Especially not a man with eyes as dark as obsidian and a heart protected by granite. A granite, she thought with a sob, she'd hoped to have chipped. She placed her hand over the crest of her bump, reassuring both herself and their baby that they'd be okay.

'It will all work out in the end,' she whispered. 'It's what Auntie Star is always saying. And Great-Great-Great-Grandmother Catherine? Trust, love and faith,' Summer assured her child, wiping away the last of her tears.

The sound of the ancient doorbell ricocheted throughout the sprawling estate that looked—at least on the outside—like Downton Abbey. On the inside? It could have inspired Dickens. For five generations the men of the Soames line had let the estate go to ruin, fruitlessly looking for the Soames diamonds. And the last, their grandfather, in his madness had been driven to knocking great holes in the walls. The irony was how close he had actually come to finding them.

Summer took a deep breath, swept another reassuring hand over her belly and whispered, 'It's time to meet your aunties.'

Summer opened the front door and was instantly

pulled into a tangle of arms that squashed and hugged and she didn't need to see her sisters' faces to know she was *home*. It didn't matter where they were in the world, as long as they were together. Summer breathed them in. She had missed them so much.

'Oh my God, it's so good to see you,' Star rushed out in one breath. 'And oh my God, we have so much to tell you, and oh my... *God, what is that?*'

Summer found herself thrust back as Star stared wide-eyed at her stomach. Over her shoulder, Skye's delighted smile followed Star's gaze down to Summer's waist and her eyes sparked with shock.

'Surprise!' Summer called weakly just before she burst into tears again.

As if the spell had been broken, Summer was instantly pulled back into her sisters' loving embrace and given soothing declarations of support and reassurance. Unfortunately, this only made her cry harder, until Skye took charge and guided them off the steps and into the estate.

They held her all the way to the Little Library, Skye on one side, Star on the other, words of love filling the cold damp estate and easing Summer's hurt just a little. Once they had seen her settled in the large wingback chair, Skye put another log on the fire and ordered Star to make a cup of herbal tea from the kettle they'd set up in the library almost two months ago.

Skye crouched down and levelled her gaze at Summer. 'Are you okay?'

Summer nodded, blushing furiously now that the crying had once again stopped.

'Is the baby okay?' Star asked from behind her sister.

Summer nodded again, her hand soothing over the crest of her bump, and when she looked back up she saw the most beautiful smiles on her sisters' faces— joy lighting their eyes, pure and bright. Summer sniffed and Star passed her a tissue, keeping one back for herself and wiping at her eyes. Summer smiled as she could see Skye trying to suppress an eye-roll at their romantic middle sister.

'Can I ask—?'

'I don't want to talk about it. Now you're here—'

'Summer,' Star chided.

'I don't,' she replied, shaking her head resolutely. 'Besides, we have to find the jewels.'

'But I thought you found the jewels?'

'I haven't actually seen them. I was waiting for you both.'

As if quickly weighing up the importance of things, Skye seemed to come to a decision. 'The diamonds aren't going to disappear overnight,' she insisted gently. 'They can wait. *You* are more important right now. And we're not going anywhere until you tell us what's going on,' she said firmly.

The kettle reached boiling point and clicked off, all the sisters' gazes called to it, and a sudden silence blanketed the room until Star laughed. 'Okay, let's have some tea, take stock and, you know, breathe.'

Skye and Summer shared a look.

'Okay, who are you and what have you done with Star?' Skye demanded.

Star smiled. 'We have a *lot* to catch up on.'

And for just a moment they enjoyed the silence, enjoyed being back together again, reunited after the longest time away from each other. Then, as Star made the tea, Skye told them about her fiancé Benoit and the cottage in the Dordogne they had been staying in for the last few weeks. Star asked a few questions before telling her own tale about the oasis the Prince of Duratra had whisked her away to before his ostentatious proposal and how much she wished she had some *qatayef* to share with them as they had their tea. It was as if they sensed that Summer needed time just to let the heavy emotions settle. Warmth finally seeped into her skin and wrapped around her heart and finally both Star and Skye looked at her expectantly.

'I don't know where to begin.' Summer shrugged helplessly.

'At the beginning, of course,' Star replied, as if she were talking to her primary school class.

Summer took a deep breath, the words rushing out on a single exhale. 'I found my dad.'

'Wait…what?' Skye asked, clearly not expecting that to be where Summer's story began.

'In Greece. I found my father.'

'But I thought Mum didn't know his name?' said Star, frowning. 'Which was why she could never find…' She trailed off, as if suddenly understanding.

'Oh, no,' Skye said. 'Really? She knew the whole time?'

Summer nodded, the ache of all those missed years, of all the questions unanswered for so long, that missing part of her… She understood *now* why her mother had done what she'd done but, with a child growing within her, she knew that she couldn't have made the same choice.

'Why didn't you tell us?' Skye asked gently.

'I didn't want you to think badly of her. *I* didn't want to think badly of her.' Summer shook her head, trying to find the words to explain why she'd hoarded that information, hoarded that hurt from her half-sisters. Skye's father had started another family after he and Mariam broke up, Star's father had died tragically when she was just months old. But Kyros? He was *her* father and a part of her feared they wouldn't understand the need she'd felt to meet him. The need in her to connect with a man she'd never met. And perhaps beneath that, deep down, the thing she hadn't been able to admit… that if he rejected her then she wouldn't have to tell them. No one would have to know.

'I… I wanted to meet him first,' Summer said.

'And did you?'

CHAPTER ONE

Five months ago...

YOU CAN DO THIS, Summer told herself as she stepped out of the air-conditioned arrivals hall in Athens and was hit by a bank of heat that nearly knocked her back. Looking out at the wide road and the bus stop, she squinted as the sun bounced off the pale concrete floor.

She stared at the instructions from her hotel—a hotel that was within walking distance of Kyros Agyros's office building—and after gazing longingly at the line of taxis she steeled herself and found the ticket machine that thankfully had an English language button.

Less than five euros and ten minutes later she was on the bus, with half her mind on the stop announcements and half a mind on her father. An ache bloomed in her heart, one that had been there ever since she'd found the photo of her parents tucked away in the attic amongst all the old albums and family documents. Mariam had always told her that she'd never known her father's last name.

Oh, she'd told Summer many other things—that his name was Kyros, that, just like her, he had a little mole on his collarbone. That he'd made her laugh, made her believe in love again, even through her grief, and, despite how brief it had been, they'd had a wonderful, magical relationship. And Summer had never doubted it. Until, when looking for her passport, she'd instead found a picture of her mother staring deep into the eyes of a handsome man—and on the back, written in her mother's handwriting, the name Kyros Agyros.

Her already shaky foundations had been rocked by the secret Mariam had kept from her and, no matter how much she wanted to ask her mum about it, she couldn't. Because Mariam Soames was ill. Very ill. Words like stage three and cancer sent tremors through her and Summer dashed away a tear that threatened to fall. So no. She couldn't ask her mum about why she'd lied about knowing her father's identity. So that only left her one other option.

'Syntagma Square,' a robotic voice announced, and Summer grabbed her large rucksack and made it off the bus just in time.

She had planned to find her hotel first. It was, according to the guide, less than a ten-minute walk south of the square. But when she turned and saw the Parliament building behind her, she lost her breath on a gasp. On the opposite side of a wide road, white columns gleamed against the burnt yellow brickwork and towered magnificently over the square. Behind her, steps led down to a fountain where kids were playing and screaming and splashing water at each other.

Off to the side were rows and rows of canopied tables and chairs, the scent of coffee hitting her all the way to where she stood.

In an instant she was filled with something she could hardly explain. Her geophysics professors and fellow students certainly would have laughed if she'd tried to explain it to them, but her heart swelled and she was brimming with something warm and thick and sweet. This was part of her culture, her heritage, her identity.

She walked across the length of the square, taking it all in. The heat, the people, the colour, the noise—it was so different to what she was used to. She was about to try and find the road that her hotel was on when she followed the sleek lines of a gleaming office building into the sky, shocked to see a bright red illuminated sign bearing her father's name.

She'd known his office was near here, but…an entire building? Her heart started to race and she rubbed her suddenly damp palms on her trousers, resenting the physical manifestation of a hormonal shift in adrenaline and cortisol. As if in defiance, Summer hitched her rucksack higher onto her shoulder and pushed her way through the circular doorway into a large atrium.

Instantly she found herself gawking as she looked up at the ceiling that reached thirty storeys up, feeling a strange sense of vertigo. The press of the air conditioning cooled the sweat slicking her skin and she resisted the urge to shiver. Summer looked to the reception desk where a beautiful dark-haired woman was waiting, her smile a slash of bright red lipstick.

'May I help you?' she said in perfect English as she approached, without Summer even having to do the awkward *Do you speak...?* dance.

Summer bit her lip, releasing it only when she finally had the courage to utter the words, 'I would like to see Mr Agyros, please.'

The receptionist hit her keyboard with a few furious strokes. 'I see, and do you have an appointment?'

'Unfortunately, no. Could you tell him that... Mariam Soames would like to see him?'

The receptionist looked at Summer, a little confused. 'I'm afraid that won't be possible.'

'I'm sorry, I know I don't have an appointment but it really is quite urgent that I speak to him.'

'I *appreciate* that, but it's not possible because he's not here. He is away with family.'

Family. The word sliced through Summer and, although she knew it was just a word, knew Kyros Agyros would have a family, it hurt unaccountably. He was supposed to be here. She'd done her research.

Her expression must have betrayed her because the receptionist was looking at her as if worried. 'Is there someone else I can put you in contact with?'

'No, thank you,' Summer said, shaking her head. 'Do you know when he'll be back?'

'I'm not at liberty to say,' the receptionist said, not unkindly.

Summer left the building feeling utterly shocked. She'd checked—he was supposed to be at a conference here in Athens according to several press releases and two different websites.

Back out on the street, the wave of heat made her feel nauseous and she sank onto the stone wall surrounding the building, trying to ease the seesawing motion the world seemed to suddenly take on. She felt so *lost*. She had wasted almost her entire savings on this trip. Savings that she'd planned to use to pay back her sisters. So *foolish*. Did she really think that… what—she'd come all the way here, head into his office, introduce herself and he'd welcome her like the long-lost daughter he'd always wanted?

The online research she'd done on Kyros had shown a lifetime of financial success stories and philanthropic endeavours, but very little about the man himself. He seemed to have kept himself out of the public eye as much as possible and the few articles she'd found indicated that he protected his privacy with two things: ruthlessness and a man called Theron Thiakos.

And as she looked up at the entrance to the building the man himself emerged from the revolving doors and Summer put her hand to the stone to steady herself. He stopped a few feet from the building to take a call. There, in the middle of the pavement, he seemed utterly heedless of the people having to swerve around him, an innate authority signalling his superiority.

She had seen pictures. Vague impressions of dark hair and formidable expressions, but at the time her attention had been on her father. Now, as she took in the entirety of Theron Thiakos, Summer lost her breath, as if the full Technicolor image was too much for her brain to handle.

Angles. Sharp, clean angles she wanted to trace with the palm of her hand. That was what Summer saw first. The wedge of his shoulders, the slant of a determined brow, the sharp cheekbones and the slash of his lips. They made her want to touch. She'd *never* felt like that before. She shook her head and tried to appraise him clinically, like the scientist she was.

He was tall, at least six foot.

Sleek. Fine.

She frowned at the useless descriptors, but they wouldn't stop coming.

Dark. Brooding.

She slowed her breathing, hoping it would help calm her erratic pulse, forcing her online research to mind. Thiakos was only six years older than her and, at twenty-eight, he had achieved a status and security that some could only dream of. He had graduated from a *very* prestigious school that counted the children of princes and diplomats amongst its alumni.

Elite.

Summer bit her lip at the rising heat on her cheeks.

After excelling in his national service with the Greek armed forces, staying for longer than the allotted time period, he had walked straight into a high-level position in Agyros's company before branching out with his own security company. Agyros had been Thiakos's first contract, but was by no means his only client. But nothing in her research of Theron Thiakos had prepared her for...*him.*

She looked down at her hands and noticed that they were fisted against her trousers, before shaking them out. By the time she looked up she couldn't see him any more. Panic rushed through her as suddenly what felt like her only connection to her father had disappeared.

The receptionist hadn't been able to tell her when her father would be back, but Theron Thiakos might.

She jumped up, blood rushing to her head as if she'd been holding her breath, and ran across the road, ignoring the blaring of car horns behind her. Careening round a corner, she caught sight of him again and the wave of relief that struck her was so powerful she sagged against the nearby building. Forcing her legs to move again, she took measured breaths, trying to slow the pulse raging in her ears, and focused her gaze squarely on his back. Her eyes tripped along the inches of his very broad shoulders and danced downward to lean hips and...

The sound of a laugh cut through her thoughts and, although it was still early, she noticed that all around them bars and cafés were bustling with people and animated conversation, the air electric and infectious. Everyone looked glamorous and sophisticated, bright and colourful and Summer felt the opposite of her namesake in black cropped chinos and a white and black striped boatneck top.

But she had learned a long time ago not to draw attention to herself. Each of the Soames girls had. It wasn't the 'done thing' to have children by three different fathers and, while no one had said anything to their faces, the whispers and drawn curtains and judgement was evident from parents, teachers and neighbours alike.

And then choosing to study science? Worse, a subject like geophysics. The first and only time she'd worn anything remotely bright to class it was as if she'd thrown potassium into water. God only knew what would happen if she'd dared to wear make-up. Or—heaven forbid—a *skirt*.

Theron Thiakos turned into a bar on the corner. Large windows had been folded back like a concertina and people spilled onto the outside seating area. It was like everything Summer had encountered so far, colourful and riotous. She watched as he was greeted by a group of friends, shaking hands and kissing cheeks, and she barely resisted the urge to rub at her own tingling cheek.

'Good evening, are you looking for a table?'

Summer's focus on Theron was such that the waiter had to repeat his question before she realised he was speaking to *her*.

'Yes.' The word jerked out of her before she could change her mind.

'Theron, what are you doing here?'

It was the second time someone had asked him the same question and, unsurprisingly, his response was the same. A tight smile reminded them that not only was he their boss and the owner of the hugely successful international company they worked for but that he didn't have to explain himself to anyone. As expected, the person who had asked the question scurried off into the crowd.

He was here precisely because he didn't want to be. It was good for him to keep himself *and* his staff on their toes. But as he accepted a drink from the waiter he couldn't block out the conversation he'd had with Kyros's niece that morning.

It's just family. I'm sure you understand.

Just family.

Family.

Four hours ago, Theron had ensured an irritated Kyros boarded the boat kept docked at Piraeus, which took him away to the 'surprise' family gathering that the Agyros clan had organised. It had been pitched as a celebration, but it was so close to the first anniversary of Althaia's death that neither man had been fooled. Kyros had left to commemorate the loss of his wife and Theron hadn't been invited.

He had watched the boat sail out from the harbour, ignoring the devastating ache deep within and instead feeding the belief that he was better off alone. Repeating that thought like a mantra in his mind, he tuned back in to the sounds of the bar. Over the low hum of voices, glass shattered, a woman screamed in delight and a man laughed. His head snapped up.

It was the tone of their laughter that gripped him. It poked and prodded at a memory from Theron's childhood—from the orphanage in the days before he'd met Kyros. From before his life had changed irrevocably. It was snide, conspiratorial, mean and it cut him like a knife.

He turned to search out the source of the laughter amongst the bar's patrons. Noticing the two younger men standing on the brink of the outdoor seating area, he followed their gaze towards a blonde rolling her shoulder as if working out a tight muscle.

His gaze stuttered over her and a sudden rush of incendiary heat poured over him. A heat that felt without beginning or end, but one most definitely with her at its focal point. She glowed, a golden halo of hair, her skin warm like the first blush of life and her lips…the kind of fresh luscious red that money couldn't buy. Hungrily, he consumed what he could see of her, gorging himself so quickly he could only take in broad strokes. He almost stepped back to sever the power of his reaction.

He forced his gaze back to the two men and it was clear. She was their intended target.

Picking up his drink, Theron pulled out his phone as if checking an email and slowly closed in on the men.

'I bet you one hundred euros that she'll spend tonight in my bed.'

'Her? Why?'

'Why not?'

All three men turned to look at her as she thanked the waiter in English and the second guy grinned. 'Two hundred says she'll be in mine.'

'Three hundred with photos,' the first said with a leer that made Theron see red.

He forced himself to loosen his grip or he'd break

his mobile. And he'd much rather break something of theirs.

He watched as the first guy made his approach, the way they tag-teamed it made Theron fear just how many times this had happened before. Surreptitiously, he took photos of both the men before putting his phone away, looking up to check the girl's reaction. They had chosen her because she was on her own, English, a tourist, a *target*.

The word ricocheted through him, bouncing off different memories from the past. In those first few months in the orphanage, he had seemed like a target to the other kids too. But he had learned and paid attention and used everything available to him so that no one considered him a target ever again. Him or those he cared about.

Through the haze of his thoughts, he felt her eyes on him, pulling him back to the present, and an unholy need exploded into being deep within him, like a punch to his gut. She held his gaze as if she was there with him, standing in the eye of the storm of need, and it was an experience unlike any he'd ever had.

And then one of the men moved between them, cutting off Theron's line of sight and taking a seat at her table. By the time he could see her again, she was smiling, her face open and curious and wholly unaware of the danger she was in. Theron rejected any further prevarication.

'Darling,' he called loudly in English as he made his way towards her table, his purpose in reaching her quite clear. A few heads at surrounding tables turned to him and as she looked up her eyes widened to near comical proportions—only there was nothing funny about the gold and green that glittered in her hazel eyes. It was such a sight he nearly stopped. But didn't.

'Sorry I'm late—forgive me?' he asked as he rounded the table and placed a kiss on her head. He felt her flinch beneath him, but he didn't give her the time to question what was going on. 'You have company?'

'Mr Thiakos,' said the first man, half rising out of his chair—to greet him or run away, it seemed the man himself wasn't sure. It wasn't unusual for strangers to recognise him, and in this instance it would make things considerably easier.

Theron held his hand out and when the man reached his out, Theron's grip would have crushed walnuts. The second man in the chair beside him rose and Theron placed his other hand heavily down on the man's shoulder and pushed him back into his seat.

'Gentlemen,' he all but snarled. To the outsider they looked like a group of friends meeting for a drink, but the undertone was as dangerous as a riptide. 'Allow me to explain,' he said in rapid Greek. 'I overheard your little *bet*.' The guy beside him jerked beneath his hand, but Theron simply held him in place. 'Now, as you can imagine, the man who wins this bet, who takes this lovely young woman to bed, will have to contend with me. Or not? I suppose, then, it could be said that *I* will win this bet, no?'

The first man paled considerably, and Theron waved off the verbal fountain of apologies that streamed forth. 'The money?' he demanded. The man's eyes flashed with anger, but Theron had seen and been worse. He simply nodded, forestalling any further objection.

The first guy reached for his pocket and pulled out two hundred euros as the second guy did the same.

'I believe it was three hundred. I have *photos*,' he said, offering his phone and displaying their images, the threat clear. After a reckless moment of deliberation, each man finally handed over three hundred euros and left.

Theron watched them until he was sure they were gone and turned back to find the blonde watching *him*. Again. As someone used to being the observer, it was a novel experience.

'Theron Thiakos,' he said, holding out a much gentler hand in greeting, wondering if she had any idea how close she'd come to a very dangerous situation.

She looked up at him with huge wide hazel eyes, not once glancing at the six hundred euros on the table. She reached out her hand and, as it slipped into his, the smooth skin gliding against his flashed the most indecent images into his head.

'Summer,' she said by way of introduction.

Heat. Warmth. The feeling of the sun against his skin.

It wasn't her name that conjured such impressions. It was *her*. He needed to leave. Theron nodded to the money on the table. 'That's yours,' he said and got up to leave.

'Why?'

It was the way she asked. As if it was completely

foreign to her that she would be given something for nothing. 'It was a con,' he bit out.

'I don't understand.'

'They had a bet as to which one could sleep with you tonight.'

The colour ran from her face, leaving her looking pale and shocked.

'They were being perfectly nice,' she said in the way that people did when they didn't want to believe they were victims.

'And take the photos to prove it,' he explained.

'And the money? That you took off them?' she demanded as if she wanted to see all the workings of what had just happened before she could believe him.

'They'll only learn if it hits them where it hurts.'

And if Theron delivered the photos to his investigative team to see if there would be enough evidence to take to the police. This probably wasn't their first time. He had turned away and was about to leave, determined not to give her another thought, when he heard what she said next.

'Thank you,' she said, sounding a little unsure if that was what she meant.

Against his will, he turned back to her. He came from a world where *thank you* was a forgotten word and the conclusion of business was the payment of an invoice. But she was looking at him as if he sat on a white horse and had just slayed a dragon. And he didn't think *anyone* had looked at him like that before.

Before he could leave, a waiter arrived with three drinks, oblivious to the disappearance of two of his customers, mainly because he was eyeing the pile of banknotes on the table. Theron resumed his seat and waited for the server to leave.

He gathered up the money and passed it to *Summer*. Her name in his mind did things that he didn't want to look at too closely.

'Please. Put this away before you draw even more unwanted attention.'

She took the handful of notes from him, blinking as if only now realising just how much it was. 'I can't take—'

'You can,' he said firmly.

The dim lighting made it impossible to tell, but he thought she might have blushed when his fingers met hers. The women he encountered didn't blush. Oh, he would leave them flushed. And panting. But...blushing spoke of innocence. An innocence he shouldn't even be in the proximity of.

'He knew you?' she asked, as if finally processing the events that had happened. 'He *recognised* you,' she said, a statement this time.

He shrugged off her apparent realisation of his notoriety, instead finding focus once again in her features. Her thoughts had furrowed her brow, drawing his attention to a nose that was distinctly 'button-like'. From there it was impossibly easy to drop his gaze to her lips and he was forced to stifle the sound of his swift inhalation.

Her lips looked swollen, as if recently kissed and thoroughly so. It wasn't a pout, and it wasn't the exaggerated bee-stung puff that silly people paid ridiculous amounts for. It was a natural fullness that he wanted to bite down gently on. There wasn't a slick of lipstick on them, yet their colour was as rich a red as his fa-vourite Limniona. He could almost taste the wine on his tongue, the scent of the herbs and cinnamon spice in the air about them.

'What are you doing here?' His question surprised them both and for the first time in a long time he felt the white-hot sting of embarrassment. Never before had he shown such a shocking disregard for self-control as to give voice to what definitely should have been a passing thought.

'I'm… I was supposed to be meeting someone.'

Her answer pierced the haze she had plunged his mind into. 'Oh, my apologies,' he said, frowning. He wasn't used to misreading situations, given that his career depended on it. 'I'll—'

'Oh, no, it's not like that,' she said, the words rush-ing out just like the hand she placed on his forearm. 'I… Family. I was supposed to be meeting family, but he's not here.'

Summer was quite aware that she was staring, but she couldn't help herself. And it had absolutely nothing to do with whether Theron Thiakos had access to her father, and everything to do with the fact that she had never seen anyone like him before.

He was impossibly good-looking. Carelessly so. Although his body was angled away from her as if he was desperate to leave, he seemed as unable to break the strange connection between them as she was.

Which was why she noticed the minute tremor that rippled beneath the surface of him when she had mentioned family. To some he might have appeared relaxed, but there was a tension formed deep within him and she didn't need a seismograph to know it. He reminded her of dolerite, the rock formed from pressurised molten lava.

'You are on your own?' He didn't seem to like the idea.

'In Greece? Yes,' she confirmed.

He turned back to his friends, his gaze snagging on the exit to the bar and then back to her, and something in her curled as she realised he didn't want to be there. With her. Shame. Embarrassment. Frustration?

She looked down as she saw him press a business card along the table with his index finger.

'Just in case you get into trouble.'

'I won't need it,' Summer said, no matter how desperate she was to accept the link to him, to her father.

He smiled, a painfully civil press of his lips that she felt around her heart. 'Maybe, maybe not. But take it so I will be able to sleep tonight.'

And with that he disappeared.

For a moment she sat, stunned, watching him leave. And only then did she realise she hadn't asked him when her father might return.

CHAPTER TWO

SUMMER HAD BEEN awake for a while without realising it. Staring up at the ceiling, her mind had continued to play out her dreams from sleeping into waking. And if it had just been a matter of images she might have been able to shake off the strange fantasies that had rolled out through the night hours. But it was the feel of them that had shaken her.

She could have sworn on the Bible that she knew the weight of his hand on her thigh, the press of his lips against her neck, the warmth of his body against hers, the safety she felt within his arms. A safety, a presence that made her unaccountably sad. The kind of deep sadness that felt familiar, that felt *old*.

Loneliness.

She realised it with a sense of confusion. She blinked at the ceiling and then approached it with a rationality that she was known for. Clearly it had more to do with missing Kyros Agyros than Theron and any such emotional reaction was surely understandable. Perhaps it was because she was in Athens alone that made it seem more…powerful.

She blinked back the threat of tears and threw herself into the shower, making plans as she washed the entirety of last night from her hair.

She didn't know when Kyros might return from wherever he was, but she had to hope that it would be before she left in a week's time. She decided to pass by the Agyros building later that afternoon and if there was a different receptionist she would try her luck again. If he hadn't returned in three days, then she would *have* to call Theron and somehow force the conversation onto her father. Until then she wanted to see as much of her heritage as possible.

After breakfast she left the hotel and decided just to walk. The streets ranged from hidden cobbled passageways littered with coffee tables, fuchsia bougainvillea and old men playing backgammon, to wide city streets that stretched for blocks and shops with expensive fashion labels and jewellery.

She wondered what her father was doing now. Was he still here in Athens? Or had he left for some other part of the world just at the exact moment she'd arrived looking for him? She tried to imagine what it might have been like to grow up here and was pierced by a sharp prick of guilt. She would never exchange what she'd had growing up with Skye and Star and her mother. Whenever she thought of Mariam her mind skittered over itself. As if she wasn't able or ready to think about how she had lied to her.

It hadn't taken much research to discover that Kyros had been married to a woman called Althaia. She had died twelve months ago and Summer had felt a strange grief on behalf of a father she had never met for a woman she had never known. They had married before Summer was born, so clearly her father and mother must have had an affair. Summer didn't know what to think about that, but wondered if it was why Mariam had never told her the name of her father.

She went to buy a bottle of water at a kiosk, pulled out her wallet and felt her eyes widen at the sight of the six hundred euros from the night before that she had completely forgotten.

Should she give it to the police? She took the change from the man at the kiosk and clamped her bag a little more tightly under her arm as she took a sip from the bottle of water. It wasn't exactly stolen though. She bit her lip and frowned. The thought of spending it made her feel a little hot around her neck—as if it were wrong. Yes, she could use it to pay for her flights or the hotel, or even a little treat, but it made her stomach squirm.

She and her sisters had always been frugal with money. They'd had to be. Mariam had provided love and security but not always consistency and over the years all three sisters had been there to fill in the gaps. But in the last few years Skye had worked as a secretary for a local builder and Star as a teaching assistant at the local primary, sharing a flat so they could help pay for the expensive tuition fees for Summer's geophysics degree. And she was determined that when she graduated and got her dream job she'd be able to give back to them.

Summer's part-time job meant that she had *some*

savings so the lure of ill-gotten gains waned considerably. And only when she saw the animal shelter on the corner did her heart ease a little and she knew what she had to do. Five minutes later and six hundred euros lighter she felt *good*. For the first time since leaving her father's office she felt...*happier*.

She passed beneath a bright white and yellow awning, absentmindedly looking at the display in the window, and stopped, staring at the most beautiful yellow dress she'd ever seen. The long-sleeved ankle-length dress was deceptively simple and utterly elegant. A button-lined deep V-neck reached tantalisingly low and hugged the torso, flaring out at the legs and making it eminently cooler than what she was currently wearing. The design was pretty but it was the colour that really caught Summer, the kind of bright sunny yellow she'd always been told that blondes could never wear. *Should* never wear.

Beyond her reflection, she saw a woman smiling at her and beckoning her into the shop. Summer was about to shake her head regretfully when she saw herself meeting her father in a dress like that. Looking beautiful and accomplished. And not like...*her* as she was now. Crumpled old clothes in muted colours. *Invisible* colours.

She did have her savings...

You can't, she told herself.

Unbidden, Theron's voice from the night before replied, insistent and final.

You can.

* * *

All morning Theron had stared at the Parthenon from his office window when he should have been answering emails, phone calls, running last month's figures or doing *anything* but thinking of an English girl waiting for her family.

He could blame it on the fact that he hadn't been with a woman for nearly eighteen months, but that would only be a half truth. Ever since he'd bought the apartment at Althaia's insistence, he'd not been able to bring a woman back there. Before her death, Althaia had asked him to stop living in the short-term rentals that had made up most of his adult life thus far. Beneath that had been the silent censure about his short-term pastimes of the female variety, but she'd been too kind to call him on it.

Stability. Kyros and Althaia had always known how important it was to him. How it was more than a desire, but a need in a life that could very much have gone the wrong way, like so many others in the orphanage had. For just a moment, a memory of the first night in that place slipped through his defences and his entire body turned to stone. In a heartbeat he'd shut it down but that tension still held in his shoulders, in his jaw.

It will be good for you, she'd said.

All the while Althaia had been trying to give him stability, knowing that her death would rob him of it. She'd even tried to get him to reach out to Lykos, but that had been a step too far.

As he looked up the hill once again, he cursed. He

needed coffee. Despite his assurance that he would only sleep well if she took his number, his dreams had been fevered images of Summer wrapped in his sheets, heated, flushed and utterly debauched. And as frustrating as those images were, he much preferred them to thoughts of the past.

Stalking from his office, he ignored the confused look of his assistant, blanked the question from his second-in-command and went for the stairs instead of the elevator, hoping to work off the nervous tension thrumming through his veins. Theron took them two at a time, his sense of urgency gaining rather than decreasing with the action.

He burst onto the pavement, sending a couple of pedestrians scattering, and made his way to the best coffee cart in the whole of Athens. He caught the eye of the mean old man who worked the cart every day of the year, rain, shine and even the occasional snow. He'd had the same coffee here every day for ten years and the old goat still growled, 'What do you want?' at him every time. It might have had something to do with how he and Lykos had once stolen a whole tray of muffins from his cart and, although he was fifteen years and several million euros away from the kid he'd once been, Theron had the sneaking suspicion that the vendor remembered it.

The rich smell of chocolatey coffee hit him and soothed this strange aimless fury unsettling him. He rolled out his shoulders and waited at one of the cheap metal tables that despite its apparent frailty—much like the coffee vendor—had somehow lasted the test of time.

His fingertips tapped out an impatient tattoo on the table top. The old man was mean, but he didn't usually make Theron wait. He turned just as the most incredible flash of yellow caught his eye. He fought against it, he tried *so* hard not to look, but the impression of supple curves outlined in gold was seared immediately and indelibly into his mind. The woman had her back to him, affording him an exquisite—if illicit—view of the way the material caressed the sweep of her backside and swayed gently as she leaned towards the coffee vendor, who looked as if he'd just fallen in love.

Theron couldn't *not* trace the arch of her spine and wonder whether the space between her shoulder blades would fit his outstretched palm perfectly. Blonde tendrils had been swept up to reveal a neck pink from the sun, but no less tempting to his lips and tongue.

She looked around too quickly for him to turn away and his gaze crashed into a gold-flecked hazel stare that instantly widened with surprise. A surprise he felt himself, down to his very soul. Her name sounded in his mind as if he hadn't already thought it a hundred times that day. But his name on her lips sent a surge of fire through his blood.

Her footsteps faltered and she came to a stop in the middle of the tables, staring at him while Theron sat there, hypnotised by the sight of her, so beautiful he felt changed by it.

Finally, he stood, pulling himself to his full height. 'Summer.'

She looked back to the coffee vendor, who shooed her in Theron's direction explaining in broken English that he'd bring her coffee over. Looking decidedly uncomfortable, she picked her way through the tables, the sway of the yellow material he wanted to feel beneath his fingertips gently billowing in her wake.

'I didn't know that you'd…'

'My office is just round the corner.'

'Of course.' The moment she said it she blushed and he couldn't quite fathom why she would think that his office would *of course* be round the corner.

She stood beside the chair he had offered her, looking at him in that way she did, until the vendor arrived with his coffee and her frappe. Theron ignored the side-eyed glare from the old man that warned him implicitly not to upset the nice English lady, and waited for Summer to sit.

He looked out to the street, but even the cars and tourists couldn't wipe the sight of the deceptively provocative V of her dress from his mind. As he turned back, he caught her averting her eyes and smiled at this strange dance happening between them.

'So. What do you do?' she asked, biting her lip immediately after the last word was out of her mouth.

And then he registered her question with slight surprise. It had been a while since someone had not known who he was, what he did. Had not known him to be joined at the hip with Kyros. It was novel.

'Security,' he replied, his natural disinclination to talk about himself cutting his words short.

'Financial?' she asked, a slight pink to her cheeks.

'No.'

The light seemed to dim from her eyes a little and he silently cursed. He was so unfamiliar with flirting. Was that what he was doing? In the past it had seemed much easier, the women more knowing and determined and he just as willing to go along with the simple sexual exchange. He had the suspicion that there was nothing simple about Summer.

'What have you done today?' he asked and she seemed relieved.

'I went to the Acropolis today. It was...' she shook her head, her eyes lit with excitement and pleasure '...incredible. The sense of history there is quite amazing. And the way that the underlying rock formations have developed...' She trailed off, biting her lip as if to stop herself from continuing.

'Yes?'

'Mmm?' she replied, as if asking a question.

'The underlying rock formations?'

'Oh, shall I continue?' she asked, surprised.

He couldn't help but laugh a little. 'Are you in the habit of pausing mid-sentence and changing the subject?'

'Well, yes, actually,' she answered honestly. 'Usually when I start to talk about rock formations, people's eyes glaze over,' she said, sweeping a loose corn-coloured tendril back behind her ear.

'Are my eyes glazed over?' he asked and held his breath as she leaned forward across the table to look more closely at his eyes, squinting and assessing and smiling as if he'd delighted her somehow.

'No,' she replied, trying and failing to contain a gentle laugh.

He gestured for her to continue, picked up his coffee and sat back in his chair to listen to her talk on, of all things, rock formations.

'It's actually quite interesting really, because the limestone capping the Acropolis—the ground on which the Parthenon is built—is Cretaceous Age Tourkovounia Formation. But the layer beneath that, the Athens Schist, is from nearly thirty million years *after*. So the upper rock layer is older than the lower, which is a perversion of the principle of superposition.'

He nearly choked on his coffee at the way she said perversion and he felt like a naughty schoolboy. He didn't think he'd *ever* felt like that, even when he had been at school.

'And because the schist is more susceptible to weathering than the upper layer of limestone, it's being nibbled away over time from the sides. But essentially it's an erosional remnant of a much larger...'

'Larger...?'

'Thrust sheet,' she said, blushing, and as much as he tried, he really couldn't help the smile that pulled at his mouth. 'I'm sorry, I should shut up,' she concluded.

'Why?' he asked, genuinely intrigued why she would regret something that brought her to life in such a way—even if he'd been amused by her accidental double-entendre. 'This is your work?'

'I'm a geophysics student. It's the study and analysis of the physical properties of the earth and space around it.'

'And your interest is in…' He had never had to work so hard to get a woman to talk to him. Instinctively, without question, he knew Althaia would have loved her.

'Well, most people go into oceanography, but I'm quite interested in engineering.' She shrugged helplessly. 'It's—' her eyes sparkled '—it's fascinating to me, but boring to most people.'

He frowned. He might not have understood all of it but her enthusiasm and expertise had been electrifying. 'Boring or intimidating?' he asked.

'Well,' she said, giving it that same kind of focused consideration he was beginning to appreciate about her, 'perhaps it's just harder to relate to,' she said, shrugging. 'Or to talk about,' she concluded.

'Or they're just not taking the time to understand why it's important to you?'

Summer's mind went completely blank. No one outside her course could relate to it and while her sisters loved her greatly and made obliging sounds and supportive gestures, they didn't know *why* it was important to her. It was something she'd never really told a soul. But the way that Theron was looking at her… expectant and…and…as if he were challenging her not to disappoint.

'I never knew my father.' His eyes flashed for a second, as if surprised at the direction of the conversation. 'It…it made me feel less…tethered. As if I wasn't quite sure of the ground beneath my feet. I have a wonderful mother and two incredible sisters,

but there was something about having half of my history, my identity, hidden that made me need to know
that everything around me is…'

'Safe,' he finished for her.

'Yes.'

He nodded. And for just a second she thought he
understood. That he knew that feeling too.

'What you do is important,' he stated and the ferocity shining in his eyes painted her skin in sparkles, the
assurance of his words vibrated in her chest, making
her feel glorious. But then he blinked and it was too
late to ask him about the hurt she had seen beneath the
burn in his eyes. He had covered it so quickly, if she
hadn't been so used to observing and recording she
might have missed it. 'Everyone in Greece knows that.'

She linked his two statements and made the connection. 'Of course. Your earthquakes here are—'

'Almost daily.' He seemed dismissive.

Summer nodded, feeling a little less shiny. She had
waited so long to find someone who was impressed by
what she did, but when it had happened, when Theron
had said those things, all she'd wanted was for him to
be impressed by *her*.

She leaned back in her chair, trying to shift away
from the gravitational field that seemed to pull her
to him. She took off the straw's paper wrapping and
plunged it into the coffee the vendor had assured her
she'd like. The moment the cool, sweet, creamy coffee
exploded on her tongue she couldn't help but moan. In
her peripheral vision she saw Theron's jaw clench and

pulse. Perhaps he believed that iced coffee was for children, she thought, but she didn't care. It was delightful.

He checked a watch that could only be described as obscenely expensive and glanced at her quickly, as if checking it was safe to do so. 'You've eaten?'

The question caught her as slightly strange. As if he didn't quite care, but wanted to make sure that she was looking after herself. She was tempted to lie, but found herself shaking her head when he returned his eyes to hers.

Then a gaze that had been distracted, as if he'd been at war with something in his thoughts, cleared and the creases at his eyes softened. 'Would you have dinner with me?'

Her mind skittered to a halt, quickly running over the last few moments. She might not be well versed in dating, but had he intended 'You've eaten?' to be an invitation? She couldn't help but smile a little at the discomfort he was hiding fairly well as she kept him waiting. A hundred reasons to refuse ran through her mind against the one that connected him to Kyros. But that wasn't the reason she placed her hand in his.

It was a little awkward at first as they made their way out of the square, past cafés and bars, weaving between pedestrians, but after a few minutes it eased and became comfortable. And then comfortable became something warmer, softer…something intangible that Summer couldn't explain or quantify, but could most definitely *feel*. She smiled and when she turned to see him casting a glance her way, the hint of something soft curling the corner of his lip, she felt it in her chest. A thud. A beat. A pulse.

When he asked, she explained a little about her family, what it was like to grow up in the New Forest, focusing on her siblings rather than her mother. The ache in her chest from the hurt and confusion over her mother's lies a bruise she gently protected. Theron was now talking about the way the different areas in Athens had changed over the years, and she wondered what he would think if she told him about Kyros. Her conscience stirred, warned her that by not telling him the truth, not telling him why she was there, she was lying to him. But, for the first time in her life, Summer ignored the rationality of her mind and followed the beat of her heart.

The sun was low in the sky by the time she saw the first glimmering shimmer of the sea. And soon they were walking along a pathway that bordered the thin strip of sand between them and the sea, towards a small white-fronted building with blue and white checked tablecloths.

'Is this where you bring all the girls?' she asked, forcing her tone to be light, but genuinely curious.

'No, I've never brought a woman here,' he said, looking as surprised by the answer as she was.

He was greeted like royalty by the staff and customers, who he waved off good-naturedly, and eventually they were led to an outdoor area where lines of fairy lights created an illuminated canopy above. She sat in the chair that Theron had pulled out for her and, before she could even take a breath, a carafe of wine had been placed beside large glasses of iced water. The waiter said something to Theron in Greek before leaving.

'You're hungry,' Theron determined.

'Starving,' she confessed. And within minutes nearly ten different plates had filled the table. Some she recognised, some she didn't, all smelling absolutely divine. Not knowing where to start, she followed Theron as, plate by plate, he dipped some of the gorgeous warm pitta into each dish.

He hardly ate a thing, while Summer seemed to taste and test everything, returning to ones that she liked in order but leaving her favourite until last—the one that made her eyes drift closed and her shoulders lower as if finally relaxing.

All afternoon he'd known that he should put her in a taxi and send her back to her hotel. But then she'd say something to make him laugh and he honestly couldn't remember the last time that had happened. Or she'd ask a question and the next thing he knew it was an hour later. Or she'd look at him in a way that convinced him she was the most innocent person he'd ever met. Everything was there on her face, each new delight, concern, question, joy, desire…

'Thank you,' she said, putting the fork down, her gaze low and her smile small but satisfied. 'So, why here?' she asked.

'The food is the best in Athens,' Theron said, speaking God's honest truth. It was also about two miles from the orphanage he'd grown up in and would probably still be leaving out food for the kids had he and

Kyros not funded a soup kitchen two corners over eight years ago.

'You must have been coming here a long time.'

'I have,' he confirmed, watching her look around at the humble restaurant in awe.

He speared some of the *xtapodi*—his favourite dish—and was just about to open his mouth when she asked, 'Did you come here with your family?'

The sharp sting cut him from head to toe. He hadn't expected it. He usually didn't get this far in conversation with anyone, let alone a woman. He blinked to wipe the haze from his eyes, mind and heart. 'No,' he said, trying to find his way back to the present. 'They died when I was five.'

Her eyes flashed to his, a sudden fierceness in her gaze as if she could personally hold back his grief, standing between him and it. Her sympathy was active, alive and pulsing and it shocked him to his core.

'I'm so sorry for your loss.' Even her condolence was defiant almost, rather than the muted sadness he'd had from others.

'It was years ago,' he dismissed and as she held his gaze something fresh came into his mind.

It was twelve months ago.

His eyes widened in shock. The sudden, completely unbidden realisation that Althaia's death had hit him just as hard as that of his parents gutted his heart. He mentally shook his head and excused himself from the table. As he stalked out towards the rear of the restaurant, he ordered himself to get a grip. When he got back to the table he'd send her on her way. He couldn't be around her. She prised things from him he usually kept locked tight. And he didn't have to be told how innocent she was. She'd blushed at the word thrust, for God's sake. He should send her home and head back into town and find someone to lose himself in.

Summer felt a presence coming towards the table, but instinctively knew it wasn't Theron.

'Good evening.'

She looked up to find a man even taller than Theron standing at a respectable distance away, as if not wanting to interrupt.

'Lykos Livas,' he said, holding out his hand for her to take. 'I'm an associate of Theron's. I hope you don't mind,' he said, placing his free hand on his heart in a gesture she was sure would have charmed a large percentage of the population. It might have worked on her too, if her mind wasn't already on *another* handsome Greek man. Her mind and her heart.

'It is sacrilege to allow a woman as beautiful as you to be here on your own,' he concluded.

The sheer ridiculousness of the line made her laugh and, to her surprise, rather than being offended, Lykos Livas seemed strangely pleased.

'Does that usually work?' she couldn't help but ask.

'Yes, actually,' he declared.

'Tourists?'

'Always,' he affirmed happily.

Summer shook his hand and felt…nothing. Not the tingles that shot up her arm every time Theron accidentally brushed her hand. Not the heart pounding, breathless feeling in her chest when she caught him looking at her that echoed deep within her until she felt as if she might explode.

'So, you work with Theron? With Kyros?' Summer asked, trying not to flinch as she said her father's name.

Lykos's silvery gaze sparkled as he held her gaze for a little too long. 'No,' he finally replied with a deadly smile. 'My millions are my own.' He looked behind him as if checking for Theron and reached into his jacket. He handed her his card. 'Just in case you ever need anything.'

'Why would I—?' she said, taking his card and, before she could stop him, he had swept up her hand, bowed and pressed his lips to the air just above her skin in a kiss right out of one of Star's historical romances.

'It was nice to meet you, Ms Soames,' he intoned and vanished as quickly as he had appeared.

Summer was still staring after his retreating form when Theron stalked over to the table with such fury she reared back.

'What did he say to you?' Theron demanded.

'What?'

'Livas. What did he say?'

'Nothing,' she said, folding Lykos's card in her palm. 'He just asked if I was alone. When I said no, he left.'

Theron stared at her, then threw some money onto the table. 'And the kiss?'

'What kiss?'

CHAPTER THREE

THERON KNEW HE was overreacting, knew absolutely one hundred per cent that he had regressed several millennia into caveman behaviour, but he couldn't help it. His blood rushed in his veins, pounded in his ears, and his inner voice had howled out the word *mine* the moment he'd seen Lykos bent over her hand.

He hadn't seen Lykos for ten years and Theron hated that his first reaction had been one of joy. And then he'd remembered. The way that Lykos had left, the argument they'd had, the demand Lykos had made. The betrayal he'd felt. He hadn't even been there for Althaia's funeral.

'He didn't kiss me—my hand, I mean.'

'I know what I saw.'

'Or you saw what he wanted you to see,' Summer replied, watching him closely. 'And, even if he had, it was just a kiss,' she said with a shrug.

'Just a kiss?' Theron demanded, horrified. 'There is no such thing as *just a kiss*,' he said, wondering what inept individuals she had been kissing to say such a thing.

And then she blushed and looked down at the table. And he knew. *None.*

How was it possible? This beautiful, vibrant, incredible woman and no one had kissed her? He stared at her as she tried to gather herself, understanding that she was embarrassed, and glared off into the ocean to give her a moment's privacy.

He cursed himself mentally. He'd known she was different from the women he had associated with in the past, but this? This was an innocence that should be well beyond his reach.

Coffee was placed on the table along with plates of baklava and Theron wavered. He desperately wanted to leave, return Summer to her hotel and never look back. But he couldn't leave her looking like that.

'He likes you,' he said to her. When Summer raised eyes full of questions, he explained. 'The owner. He only ever gives out one piece,' he said, pointing to the two squares of baklava on her plate.

His answer took away some of the hurt in her eyes and he was thankful. But he still marvelled at her innocence. How she could—

'The town I grew up in is quite judgemental and, my sisters and I, we have…we have different fathers. So…' she shrugged, as if that would make all the preconceptions, judgement and sadness he imagined she must have battled as a child just disappear '…for the most part people avoided us.'

'For the most part?'

She frowned, making him want to smooth away the little furrow in her brow. 'When I was about thirteen, a boy—*the* boy—at school asked to meet me after class.' She smiled sadly at herself as if she should have known better. 'I overheard his friends talking about it. How they wanted to see if I was just like my mother.'

Theron clenched his fists under the table, feeling the anger he'd banked ignite instantly, her experience with bullies and teasing melding a little with some of his own. The fights he'd had, before Lykos.

'I left him waiting and ignored him and his friends for the rest of the year.'

He tried to let go of it—the anger—the way she seemed to have done.

'It was easier to stay away from boys like that. And at uni the guys on my course… Well, they tend to be more interested in…'

'Igneous rock formations?' he asked, thinking of her studies.

She laughed, as if it was funny that she had so little experience of receiving attention, and his heart broke a little. 'Yes. Exactly,' she affirmed.

He nodded. 'Eat your baklava,' he commanded.

'Yes, sir,' she replied with a smile.

From the first mouthful of the sweet, nutty, sticky dessert she had fallen instantly in love. And through every subsequent bite Theron had sat back in his chair, sipping at his coffee, never once taking his eyes off her.

At first it had made her self-conscious. Her forkfuls had been small, dainty and her eyes low on the table. But then she had lost herself in the tastes and textures of each mouthful, caught herself stifling a moan of sheer delight and risked a glance at Theron, who seemed almost carved from stone. Almost, because there was nothing inert about his eyes. They flashed, sparked, flared, flickered... There was such movement in them she could look at them for ever. She felt them graze over her face, her shoulders, her hands where they picked up the fork, her chest when she sucked in a breath, her neck when she leaned forward to take a sip of coffee, her lips when her tongue smoothed over a drop of syrup. Every single action made her aware of her heart beating in her chest and the low pulse between her legs. Something was building within her, a yearning, a need, and she felt as if she might jump out of her own skin if it wasn't let loose. She might never have experienced it, but she knew exactly what it was. She put her fork down, giving up on the unfinished dessert because that wasn't the kind of hunger she felt now.

She knew it. And so did he.

Theron reached across the table and picked up her hand. He brought it towards him and her heart shifted. He cradled it within his palm, the pad of his thumb smoothing imaginary lines on the back of her hand as if slowly, inch by inch, he was erasing the memory of one man and imprinting himself in its place.

He lowered his head and she felt sparks ricochet in the air between his lips and her skin, the vibrations getting quicker and quicker until her heart felt as if it might burst from her chest. As his lips pressed against her skin, her heart missed a beat, her fingers curled in his palm, tightening around his hand and her thighs pulled together. She bit her lip and felt unaccountably angry when he finally released the press of his lips and looked up at her.

Just a kiss?

He had proved her wrong. They both knew it, but in doing so he'd opened a door that she'd never walked through before, never wanted to before. And now... now she feared he might close that door before she'd even tried.

Now *she* was angry. With him because she knew Theron wanted to walk away. With her father for not being there. Angry for him and for the loss of his parents. Angry with her mother for being ill. With everything *not* going to plan.

She lurched up from the table, startling him and the other customers with the scratch of the chair legs against the floor, and turned, running down the stairs and out onto the walkway illuminated solely by the light of the moon.

She called herself all the different kinds of fool she could think of. How had she let this happen? She pressed the back of her hand against her lips, as if somehow she could superimpose his kiss onto her mouth. But it only left an aching emptiness inside that hurt even more now she knew what it was like to feel filled with need and desire. Her breath sobbed against her hand and she tried to hold in the tears that wanted to be let free.

She drew to a halt, staring out at the inky black sea merging with the night, wishing for something she couldn't put words to. Fingers wrapped gently around her wrist and pulled her round and when she refused to look up into the dark expressive eyes she knew would be there, a finger hooked her chin and tilted her face to his. Eyes flickered back and forth over her face, as if trying to read thoughts that were incoherent even to her. She felt as if he were turning the pages of her mind, reading the words of her heart: desire, need, desperation, sadness, fear, yearning, permission, consent. It was there, all of it, and she just wanted him to—

He moved so slowly she thought she'd imagined it at first. She'd expected him to crush her to him, like the romances her sister Star was always swooning over. But he didn't. And somehow it was so much *more*.

She was sick with want and it took her a moment to realise it wasn't just her that felt that way. He reached up to brush a lock of hair back behind her ear, his fingers shaking ever so slightly. The moment he noticed it he clenched his fist and looked at her accusingly, as if demanding to know what she was doing to him.

Before he could take it back or change his mind, Summer closed the imperceptible distance between their lips—a space that felt like a heartbeat between before and after and…

Oh…

That was what it was like.

She'd expected his lips to feel firm and a little cool perhaps, but they were soft and so warm and sent fireworks shooting through her entire body. It was such a shock that her mouth opened on a gasp just as he began to kiss her back and the feel of his tongue gently pressing against the curve of her top lip made her breath hitch and her hands curl and, before she knew it, she had risen up onto her toes and pressed herself against the length of him and leaned into everything she was feeling.

But it was nothing compared to what she felt when he took over the kiss.

He'd given her a chance to explore, to feel, to touch, slide and press her way through it. And then he moved. His hand cradled her neck as his fingers threaded through her hair, sending the band holding it in place flying and the tendrils of her long hair falling down her back.

His other hand cupped her jaw, angling her head and her mouth in the most perfect way. Her chest rose to meet his, wanting to feel him against her, skin to skin—needing to. She reached up to clutch the lapels of his jacket, pulling them closer together. His hand slipped from her neck to her back, his fingers stretching between her shoulder blades, and she felt him sigh.

He pulled back from the kiss and pressed his forehead to hers, their rushed breathing buffeting the air between them.

This was it. This was the moment he would leave. Summer's fingers clenched reflexively. She swallowed the hurt she felt already.

'I should take you back to your hotel.'

'Should you?'

'Summer—'

Unwelcome nausea swelled in her stomach, her inner voice already howling at what he was taking away from her.

'Is this the bit where you tell me that I'm too innocent to know what I want?' she demanded. He pulled back, searching her face, and she raged at him for underestimating her. For denying her something she could see that he wanted too. 'The bit where you tell me that you're not good enough for me?'

His eyes darkened, whether in defiance or defence, she couldn't tell. And then he let her go, turned back onto the walkway and began to disappear into the night. Summer clenched her jaw, all the feelings within her bubbling up to the surface, hot, angry and aching.

'You're not that much older than me, you know,' she called after him. 'And…and…' He paused, as if wanting to hear what she was going to say. 'And you were a virgin once too!' she yelled, shocked by her own audacity.

He spun round and ducked slightly, as if to avoid the words, and closed the distance between them in seconds. '*Éleos*, will you keep your voice down?' he growled, casting wary glares left and right. He looked like an angry schoolboy, a dark curl having fallen onto his forehead and a ruddy streak on either cheek. It was comical, the laugh rising up in her chest cutting through the darker emotions from just moments before.

'Are you blushing? Was it the word virgin?' she demanded, incredulous.

'Oh, for the love of—'

He kissed her then, the way she'd thought he might but could never have expected. The crush of his lips, his body dominating hers, overpowering her and it was incredible. It was all she could do to hold onto him and not be swept away into the sea.

'You're going to ruin me, aren't you?' he asked between kisses.

'Isn't it supposed to be the other way round?' she asked, the breathlessness of her voice causing his pupils to flare. She loved being able to see the reaction in him, to know that she was the cause.

'Come with me?' he asked.

The drive they took back to his apartment was short but interminable. Nothing was said, but it was far from silent. Sitting beside her in the back seat, Theron watched her for the entire journey, his eyes conveying more than words could as they touched every part of her in a caress that she could feel. It stoked an arousal within her so strong, so pure, and the curve of his lips told her that he knew *exactly* what he was doing. Was purposely doing. And Summer gave up any concerns or embarrassment, his clear desire of her as sure a thing as she'd ever known.

He paid the driver and led her through the foyer and into the elevator, up to his apartment, and gestured for her to pass the threshold first. All the while her eyes were unseeing and her senses heightened.

He stalked her through his apartment. He hadn't turned on the lights, so only the glow of the moonlight pouring in through the glass walls spanning the length of his corner apartment illuminated her path. She was breathless with delight and dizzy with need, adrenaline coursing through her veins making her pulse trip.

The gleam in his eyes told her he felt it too. Fed from it even. Summer kicked her shoes off and into the corner of the living area as she rounded the sofa and her jaw dropped as Theron simply stepped up onto the cushions and over the back, reaching for her, but she twisted and spun away from his hold with a laugh.

She reached out to the door frame of another room and paused on the threshold as she realised it was his bedroom. Her heart pounded in her chest as she felt him behind her. He leant against the frame, his hand just inches above hers, the warmth from his body crashing against hers in waves as she took in the sight of the large bed. The throbbing of her heart radiated outwards through her entire body and she was filled with desire and need.

'We don't have to do anything you don't—'

She turned and kissed him. To stop his words, to stop the awkwardness she feared was replacing the delighted fizz from mere moments ago. She felt the curve of his lips through the kiss and he gently pulled away, softening his retreat. She couldn't quite explain the writhing emotions twisting in her because it wasn't that she was unsure, it was as if she felt embarrassed by it, even though rationally she knew she shouldn't be.

'Summer, consent is an important conversation to have,' he said, his words whispered into her ear, brushing against her neck and filling her with want. 'It's not embarrassing. It's respectful. You have as much control in this as me, and if you want to spend the entire evening making love I will. And if you want me to stop I will.' He shrugged as if it were that simple.

Summer turned, touched so deeply by his words, his assurance not only sweeping aside the awkwardness she'd felt but making her want him more, making her feel protected and cared for in a way that was somehow more than just moments before. She knew then she'd never regret tonight.

'This is something I want very much,' she said, reaching up to cup his jaw. 'And something I've only ever wanted with you. So, I do want you to stop...' she said, Theron's nod swift and sure against her palm, '...*talking*,' she finished and pulled him to her in a kiss that took him only a second to take over.

His hands settled over Summer's body, reaching for her waist and lifting her up above him so that her hair fell about them. He locked his arms around her thighs and walked them back to the bed, turning so that when they fell he was beneath her, cushioning her as she became a tangled mess of laughter and legs and arms that turned into kisses and sighs and touches that made his heart soar in a way he couldn't remember ever having felt.

'You are so beautiful,' he said, reaching up to tuck a long blonde tendril behind her ear so he could see the golden flecks in her hazel eyes. 'You should always be in this colour.'

She bit her lip as if embarrassed by his observation, but the blush on her cheeks, the widening of her eyes... He'd pay her compliments until she got used to them, until she welcomed each and every one of them as her due.

He reached for the zip he'd noticed at the side of the dress and slowly pulled it down, his fingers impatient, dipping between the opening and casting circles over smooth skin. She was exquisite. Every touch new, every taste incredible, and if this was ruin then he would go to it willingly and gladly.

She shrugged out of the top of her dress, her arms slipping through the material while holding it to her chest. He could see her nerves but he could also see her desire, her determination and when she let the top go, revealing herself to him, it made him feel so damn honoured. She bent down at the same time as he reached up towards her and they met in an axis point of pleasure and need, and as she rocked against him his pulse roared and his heart leapt.

His arms wrapped around her waist and he pulled her beneath him, drawing the dress down her hips and away from her ankles. He made quick work of his own clothes, hating to leave her even for that short time, but the way her eyes flashed and flickered all over his body was worth every second.

It was as if she were studying and analysing every inch of him and he let her, beginning to understand that it was part of her process, working through variables and collecting data. He retrieved the condom from his wallet, tore across the seal and rolled the latex over himself, her hot eyes not leaving him for a second, turning him on even more.

He placed his hands on her thighs, gently sweeping caresses inch by inch towards the apex of her legs. 'This may hurt.' She nodded, her expression serious, understanding that it wasn't his intention to. 'And know that I will stop at any time. Any, okay? Nothing is too late, or too far.'

She nodded again and he almost groaned out loud. The look in her eyes was his undoing. He leaned forward and pressed open-mouthed kisses to her neck. 'I need to hear you say it, *agápi mou*,' he whispered.

'Yes, Theron. Yes. Please... I want...' she trailed off and the yearning in her hazel gaze exploded like starbursts '...everything,' she finished, as if confused by her own desires. He wanted that for her. He wanted to scoop up the world and give it to her.

He kissed along her collarbone, his gaze snaring on a mole about two inches from her clavicle. He pressed his thumb over it, something jarring in his mind, before she shifted beneath him, beckoning his touch to the valley between her breasts. He kissed back up the long column of her neck and positioned himself between her legs. He longed to taste her, but this wasn't about his wants. He trailed his hand over her thigh and between her legs the evidence of her need, the slickness dampening the curls made his heart stop.

He bit his lip, grounding the need for control with every ounce of his intent, and as he locked his longing gaze on hers he slowly pressed into her, consuming her gasp with a kiss. He held himself still as she tensed, her eyes flaring wide with the shock, and his eyes held only regret and hope that it would pass for her quickly. She blinked slowly, breathing through it, her body beginning to relax around his. He pressed kisses against her skin, showered her in words he had no hope of her understanding, and slowly began to move within her. Bit by bit her body began to move with his, her thighs hitching around his hips, her ankles crossing behind him, pressing him closer to her, and his heart began to pound. He braced himself, his hands either side of her on the mattress, his muscles beginning to shake as he fought to control the desire that was spinning out of his reach. As if Summer felt it too, her sighs became cries of pleasure, urging him to some impossible point. Sweat-slicked and on a knife's edge, he held them at the absolute pinnacle until her release urged his own and, together, they fell deep into the night.

Summer woke the next morning encircled in Theron's arms and decided there was no better feeling than that. A blush heated her cheeks at the way he had drawn from her a pleasure she'd never known existed. She ducked beneath the covers, hiding the smile that felt private yet utterly full of joy behind the cotton. It felt... magical to be with Theron here, in this way.

But, as wonderful as it was, she knew she'd not be able to get back to sleep, so she slipped out from under his arm, tiptoed to the bathroom and turned on the shower. She threw a look in the mirror, wondering who the beautiful woman staring back at her was. The one with pink cheeks, bright eyes and thoroughly kissed lips.

Ducking beneath the powerful spray of the water, she wondered what they might do today. Maybe Theron could take her to somewhere only he knew.

Maybe, she thought, she could tell him about Kyros.
It was crazy to think that she could trust him with her
body, but not that…

Theron was still asleep when she came out, so she
grabbed a shirt from his closet, her dress now completely crumpled on the floor, and quietly stepped
out of the room. She went to the kitchen and spied a
very fancy coffee machine that only took her fifteen
minutes of opening drawers, pressing buttons, cursing under her breath and one hair pull to produce a
decent espresso.

She took the cup over to the large window that led
onto a beautiful balcony, staring at the way the sun
swept up from the sea, casting the sky in orange and
yellow hues that had her so mesmerised she didn't hear
the key in the door before it was too late.

She spun round, nearly spilling the coffee over the
borrowed shirt, and stared.

'Theron!' yelled the man with shocking white hair,
deeply tanned, lined skin and a scowl. 'Theron?'

Summer didn't recognise the rest because it was in
Greek, but she certainly recognised the man. It was
her father. Two steps brought Kyros Agyros into the
apartment enough to see her standing by the window
and close enough to break her heart.

The look he cast her was barely a sneer, the distaste in the gaze he raked over her cut her deeply and
brought a sheen to her eyes that she feared might fall
down her cheeks. Turning her back to him, she bit
her lip so hard from trying not to cry out, she tasted
blood. Her breath shuddered out of her lungs as she

heard Theron emerge from the room, throwing back to Kyros whatever response was needed. She tried to tell herself that her father didn't know, that she didn't feel mortified, humiliated or shaken, but she couldn't.

Summer held her breath through the short exchange and let it go only when Kyros had left the apartment. But something had changed. Something irrevocable. She turned, blinking away the sheen, to find Theron standing there in his trousers from last night and nothing else. He was staring at her and, no matter how much she tried to hide it, he'd seen enough.

'Care to explain to me what that was about?' he demanded, doing up the button above his trouser zip without taking his eyes off her.

'I don't know—'

'Don't lie to me.' His voice might not have been a shout, but the tone was cold and harsh in a way she'd have thought impossible after last night.

'It's hard to explain,' she replied, suddenly realising how it might look to Theron. She'd thought she'd have time. Time to explain herself.

'You are articulate and intelligent. Try.'

Summer breathed deeply. 'He's my father.'

Every single emotion that had been shining in his eyes was immediately blanked. He uttered what could only be a curse and sent a glare her way. 'Don't be ridiculous,' he all but spat.

'He is,' she insisted. 'I—'

He threw up a hand, cutting her off before she could explain. 'Of all the schemes and lies you could have told to have me even *half* believing you?' His gaze

was frigid, disgusted and horribly like the one Kyros
had spared her. He shook his head. 'No. That is the
one that would *never* work. Kyros was absolutely one
hundred per cent committed to his wife and family. I
know this to be true. I have seen it with my own eyes.'
His accent grew thicker and heavier the more vehe-
ment he became. 'So, what, this was a shakedown?'
he demanded.

'No!' Summer cried, appalled at how he'd inter-
preted the situation.

'A money-making scheme? Coming here after his
wife's death—'

'I didn't—'

'And sex with me was—what? A perk? An in?'
Theron yelled, before slamming his mouth shut as if
to prevent anything worse from coming out. Not that
Summer could even begin to imagine what that might
be.

'Did you know who I was?'

Shock pooled the blood in her stomach, leaving her
face cold. 'Theron—'

'That first night in the bar. Did you know who I
was?' he said, taking one step towards her and then
holding himself back.

The anger, the betrayal, the pain. She could see it.
Familiar as it was to the way she had felt when she'd
discovered her mother had lied to her about her father. Regret and hurt washed over her in a tidal wave,
threatening to pull her under.

'I tell you what,' he said, sniffing and walking past
her to the coffee machine. 'I'll give you fifteen minutes

to get out. And that is purely a *professional* courtesy. You were incredibly convincing last night, *agápi mou*, I must say. I am man enough to admit I fell for it,' he said, his back to her, before turning and clapping his hands together slowly.

'Well done. Now get out.'

Last night...

The noise of the bar in Mayfair cut through the haze of anger that Theron felt as if it were only yesterday rather than five months ago.

Lykos cursed. 'That was low, Theron. And, coming from me, that's saying something,' he said, disgust heavy in the air between them.

Theron felt the thick slide of shame in his gut and he took a mouthful of whisky to drown it out, not sure that it was any better than the rage he'd felt burning a hole in his heart when she'd left his apartment in Piraeus five months ago. Or the devastation he'd experienced four hours ago when she'd stood on the steps of an estate in Norfolk, staring at him in the rear-view mirror.

'I thought she was trying to get to—'

'Your precious Kyros. I know,' Lykos said as if tired of repeating himself.

'It's my job!' Theron growled.

'You keep telling yourself that.'

'What's that supposed to mean?' Theron demanded furiously.

'It means that you've always put him on a pedestal.

You've idolised him. And you'd do anything for him, no matter what it cost you. And that's not the way to live a life, Theron.'

'He stayed. Not even *you* did that,' Theron accused.

'I asked you to come with me, Theron. You made your choice. Do us both a favour, be a big boy and live with it, okay?'

'I want you to tell me what Kyros did that was *so* bad that it erased all the money, time and effort he chose to pour into us? He gave us somewhere safe from looking over our shoulder every two minutes, he gave us an education, somewhere with food we didn't have to steal.' Theron stared at Lykos, searching his features for something other than anger and disdain— searching for a trace of the man he'd grown up with, the man he'd once called brother. Before he had left him without a second glance. 'All I know is that one day you were working for him, and the next you were telling me you were going to leave. What happened? What did he ask you to do?'

But Lykos just shook his head, holding and hoarding his secrets, as he always had. He signalled to the waitress and turned back to Theron. 'So let me guess. Summer left your apartment and you went back to work as if nothing had happened, right? Did you even tell Kyros?' Lykos asked.

'What, that I had let some con artist into my bed? That as the owner of the company he uses for security, I had nearly left him open to that?'

Theron felt Lykos's silvery glare through the darkness of the bar. 'And you didn't suspect anything beyond that?'

'I didn't think of her at all,' Theron lied. 'Until you called.'

'Here,' Star eased the cup from Summer's shaking grasp, put it on the floor and took her hands in her own. 'I'm so sorry that happened to you. That you shared something so special with Theron and that he didn't believe you...'

'I'm calling Benoit. We'll do a background check on him or something. Find a way to—'

'It's okay,' Summer interrupted with a watery smile and a sad laugh. 'I'm not finished yet.' Star reached for a couple of blankets as Skye threw another log on the fire and they settled in. 'I went back to uni, not telling anyone about what happened in Greece. I thought it would be better if I forgot the whole thing and I decided I never wanted to see my father again.'

'Oh, no, Summer, you can't hold that one moment against him. I'm sure there was something else going on,' Star said, ever hopeful, always loving.

She shrugged. 'I couldn't forget the disdain in his eyes. He barely even looked at me. And what proof did I have, really? A name, a photograph, the story of a matching mole?'

'There are DNA tests that we could get,' Star offered.

'Well, that wasn't the test I ended up doing back then,' Summer confessed, remembering sitting on the bathroom floor of her room in the university halls, her back against the door and her knees pulled up to her chest, numb with shock, staring at the little blue tick.

She'd thought it was the flu. She'd felt rundown, achy, nauseous. It could have been any number of things. And then one of the guys in her class had made a stupid joke about nausea and pregnancy and, as she'd stood there smiling while everyone laughed, she'd been doing the maths. She'd been working out just when her last period had been and her world had morphed into something she barely recognised.

She'd bought a pregnancy test immediately after class and taken it the moment she'd got back to her room. Waiting for the results, she'd wanted to call her sisters…but also hadn't. She'd thought about calling Theron, but his slow clap had rung in her ears as the seconds passed. She'd left his apartment that day, eyes blinded by hot tears and cheeks stained red by hurt and guilt.

Guilt because he'd been right. She had lied to him, she had intended to use him to find out about her father. But that had been before Theron had looked at her and she'd felt *seen*. So to have that taken away when he'd refused to believe or even hear her about her father had felt like an eclipse. A sudden absence of light. And ever since she'd left Greece there had been an ache in her heart that she'd tried to blame on the disappointment of meeting her father, but she'd known that was a lie.

And in that instant she'd made a promise to her unborn child. Never would they feel rejection. Never would they feel the shame and confusion and sadness that she had experienced. And, sitting on the cold laminate floor as the blue cross had appeared, something had stirred deep within. A maternal instinct she'd never known she had. It was fierce and true and surer than anything she'd ever felt before. And it had only grown bit by bit each day since. There had not even been a second when Summer considered anything but having her child. But that didn't mean it hadn't plunged her into a state of worry and confusion.

'And within days of finding out, we were told that the NHS were unable to offer Mum's cancer treatment, Elias died and we came here for his funeral. And then, when his will dictated the search for the Soames diamonds...'

'Did you call Theron?'

'I wanted to. But I was pretty sure he'd want a paternity test and I didn't want to risk any harm to the baby. He thought the worst of me already, so I was going to wait.'

'Going to?'

'It didn't quite work out like that.'

CHAPTER FOUR

Six days ago...

THERON FISTED HIS HANDS in his trouser pockets and stared up at the Acropolis, thinking of hazel eyes, blonde hair and a yellow dress. His notoriously lethal focus had drifted in the last few months and Kyros had noticed. Theron had felt a wave of guilt each time he'd avoided the older man's probing questions. Guilt and shame that he'd been taken in by such a con. But each night as he reran the events of that morning through his mind, he came back to the same question. Summer had admitted that she'd known who he was with the same open expression as when she'd insisted Kyros was her father. An open honesty that had bewitched him from the first moment.

Had she been telling the truth?

It had driven him mad in the days and weeks following. And more times than he'd care to admit, he'd been on the verge of asking Kyros about it. About her. About whether Kyros had cheated on his wife while she'd been on her sickbed. The thought made him more furious than he'd been in years. But still, he couldn't risk it. Kyros was everything to him. He'd given Kyros his word, his loyalty, and in return Kyros had given him stability, security and a home. Theron owed Kyros that trust.

A knock on the office door cut through his thoughts, causing him to turn.

'I'm sorry, Mr Thiakos, you didn't answer your...' His secretary appeared, red-cheeked, reluctant to call him on his ineptitude. 'Mr Livas on line two for you. Would you like me to tell him you're not available?'

Lykos hadn't been in this building for nearly ten years but his reputation still stalked the halls. Theron frowned, something swift and sharp twisting in his side. Whatever it was, it couldn't be good. He picked up the phone.

'What do you want?' Theron demanded as his secretary retreated from the room.

'Lykos! Great to hear from you after all these years! You well? I *am*, thank you, Theron. And how are you? Oh, can't complain. Can't complain.' Lykos performed his one-man show through the earpiece replete with intonations worthy of an Oscar.

'Really? This is what you waste my time with?' Theron bit back angrily.

'Is it so surprising that I might want to check in on my oldest and bestest friend?' Lykos's saccharine tone made Theron's teeth ache.

'Given that it would be the first time in nearly ten years? Yes,' Theron admitted.

'Well, I've just been presented with an interesting business opportunity but... I don't know, there's something about it...'

'You're worse than a cat with a mouse. Stop toying with me and spit it out.'

'But where's the fun in that?'

'About as much fun as me hanging up on you,' warned Theron, preparing to do just that.

'Wait!'

Theron didn't say anything.

'It's a business opportunity in Norfolk.'

'You're in America?' Theron asked, confused.

'No, Norfolk, England. An acquaintance of ours brought it to me.'

'We don't have mutual acquaintances,' he growled, his voice one hundred per cent sure, but his mind flashed onto Summer looking up as Lykos bent over her hand. How had he forgotten that?

'Oh. My mistake. I must have been confused.'

'Stop being coy. You don't get confused,' Theron bit, a dangerous edge to his voice now.

'Small, blonde. Very pretty—positively *radiant*. Must say, fits her name perfectly.'

Theron gripped the phone. 'What is she doing with you?' he demanded, shocked by the phosphoric fury burning in his veins.

'Get your mind out of the gutter. It was a business proposition,' Lykos replied, distaste heavy in his tone.

'And you never mix business with pleasure?' Theron scoffed.

'Oh, all the time,' Lykos replied easily. 'I just don't mix *my* pleasure with *yours*.'

Theron breathed his heartbeat into submission. 'Has she mentioned Kyros?'

'Not once. Why?' Lykos replied.

'Are you sure?'

'It's possible that it slipped my mind,' he taunted.

'What was the business?'

'She has a twelve-million-pound estate in Norfolk she wants to sell for a third of that value.'

Theron cursed. 'She's a student. Where the hell would she get an estate from?'

'If you want to know, go ask her. Though might I suggest, before you go in there bashing down the front door—'

'No,' Theron interrupted, the sudden need to find out exactly what was going on, intoxicating. 'I don't know what the hell you're getting out of this, but I know you have an angle here somewhere. So, no, you can't suggest a thing. I'm going to get to the bottom of this *right now*. And you will *not* buy that estate,' Theron commanded.

Less than twenty-four hours later, as Theron put the rental car into park, he told himself that his pulse was pounding because of the near miss with a scaffolding lorry, *not* because Summer Soames was hiding somewhere inside the estate in front of him. What was her angle here? Had she moved on from Kyros? Was she now targeting Lykos? He could have her.

No!

Everything in him roared denial at the bitterly careless thought. He could lie and claim not to have dreamed about her every night since she'd left his bed. He could try to tell himself that he'd put her out of his mind as the money-grabbing con artist he'd accused her of being, instead of remembering the devastation in her eyes that morning, first with Kyros and then with him. But he wouldn't lie to himself about how much he'd wanted her with every single fibre of his being since that morning.

So, no. Lykos couldn't *have her*. Because Theron wasn't done with her yet. He needed to know what she was doing and whether it had anything to do with the man he would protect with his life if need be.

His shoes crunched on the gravel as he got out of the car. He had to crane his neck to take in the sprawling building, little more than a dark outline against the dusk. In the evening's gloom it was clear the estate was in need of some serious repair, but it was still a thing of beauty, faded or otherwise. There was a sense of something more, though, tugging at him, drawing him closer…but he shook the silliness out of his head as he took the steps two at a time, reaching the semi-circular dais at the top in front of a very large wooden door.

He pounded on it, wondering whether he had a hope in hell of her hearing it. As the minutes ticked by, Theron became increasingly frustrated. He stepped back off the steps and peered up at windows caked in grime and cobwebs. He frowned. The building looked deserted. Abandoned. Anything could happen here and no one would know. An icy tendril wound its way up his spine and he was worried. Worried about Summer. The suddenly frantic beat of his heart infected his thoughts and his mind quickly became a jumble so that when the door opened and he saw Summer standing there it took him a moment to breathe.

And he forgot. Forgot about Kyros and about her insane accusation. He forgot the anger that had so cleverly laid over the hurt. The ache that she'd fooled him. That she'd used him. And instead he just took her in.

A wave of relief washed over him, and a feeling he barely recognised and dared not name was left on the shore of his heart. Summer's eyes widened in recognition, and for just a second he thought he might have seen something like hope spark in her eyes.

As if tethered to her he approached her with one step. And then another. And another until somehow he was within an inch of her and his hands were reaching to frame her face and his mouth was claiming hers and he felt as if he was *home*.

A moan sounded on the air between them and he couldn't be sure if it had been hers or his. Her lips tasted of honey and opened beneath his and a shocking heat unfurled within him, his heart in his mouth and realisation on his tongue. He'd been lying to himself for months. He'd not put her out of his mind, he'd kept her there, the memories of her locked away, and the moment that he'd seen her again they were all unleashed. This was what he'd needed, just so he could breathe, he thought as he pulled her flush against his body and…stopped.

He opened his eyes to find hers staring at him, shock and something horrifyingly like fear sparking to life in them. He pulled back and reached out at the same time, his hand unerringly finding the curve, not of her stomach but a bump. Just about the right size for a…

Summer closed her eyes. It had taken her only seconds to consume the sight of him. The thick wave of hair, so dark it looked velvety, the stubble on his jaw, the breadth of his shoulders, the way his forearms corded beneath rolled-up shirtsleeves—everything about him made her want to touch. Her breathing hitched and she felt utterly betrayed by her body as it throbbed and pulsed just at the sight of him. And the thread of hope she'd barely admitted to herself during the last weeks and months sprang to life. But when he'd reached for her, hopes, fears and fantasies had disappeared and she'd melted into him as if nothing else mattered.

She'd forgotten. That was the power he had over her. For just a second of madness, she'd forgotten. Until Theron had reared back, the look of shock on his features indelibly marked across her heart.

'No.'

The word severed the spell he'd cast over her, bringing her back to reality with a painful jolt. She was surprised that it hurt so much. His denial. It wasn't as if she hadn't expected it. Neither could she blame him— she'd had that moment too. The moment when in less than a heartbeat her mind had travelled through infinite possibilities and futures, all twisting and turning out of reach in light of the shocking fact that she was now going to be a parent. But she'd also seen futures in which their child was the most precious, beautiful part of her life.

But the look in his eyes—the one he was trying so desperately to mask—was all too familiar to her and just as painful as it had been in Greece. That moment of rejection, that feeling, compounded by her father's dismissal, fired a kiln that forged steel within her. She would not subject her child to that now or ever.

'You are pregnant?'

'Yes,' she said, waiting for some kind of indication that he had realised that he was a father. But where once she had marvelled at his impenetrable, stone-like qualities, now it just felt cruel. As if it made her even more conscious of their differences. She felt soft and sore and emotional and he seemed hard, cold, tough and it made her hurt even more. What kind of father would he be for their child?

'What are you doing here?' she asked, her thoughts making her voice a whisper.

Theron blinked, looking around as if he didn't know how to answer that question. He went to say something and had to clear his throat. 'Lykos...'

Summer rolled her eyes. She should have known the Greek billionaire friend of Theron's wouldn't have kept his mouth shut. Not that she'd had much of a choice. It wasn't as if as a geophysics student she knew *that* many billionaires. And when she and her sisters had realised they would need to sell the Soames estate, and sell it quickly, Summer had remembered what Lykos Livas had said when he'd handed over his card. *Just in case you ever need anything.* Lykos had been there for her when she'd needed it, not Theron. Not the man who had tossed her from his apartment in such a cruel way.

Hurt fired her fury as she focused back on Theron, who was staring at her stomach. 'I don't have time for this,' she said around his silence. 'I don't have time for *you*. You can go,' she dismissed, her heart breaking as she turned blindly down a hallway, not caring where she went.

'I'm not going anywhere.' The tone of Theron's voice was all the warning she got before he pulled her round to face him and in an instant she was overwhelmed with the memory of the first time he'd kissed her. She looked up just in time to see the flare of his pupils as if he too was lost in the same thought. But then he blinked and once again she was shut out and the icy-cold stare he levelled at her made her shiver.

'Ask me,' she demanded.

For a second he looked confused. 'Ask you what?'

Summer shook her head, blinking furiously, praying that she could get through this before the tears came. She looked up at him, her heart breaking. 'Ask me if it's yours.'

Shock slashed angry red marks across his cheeks and gutted his chest. That was what it felt like. As if everything inside him had been scooped out and exposed.

He was more certain that she was pregnant with his child than anything he'd ever known in his entire life. The question hadn't even crossed his mind, let alone formed into a sentence, and the thought that she'd believe he'd question such a thing burned his soul.

You were incredibly convincing last night, agápi mou, I must say. I am man enough to admit I fell for it.

This time the slow clap that echoed in his mind was for him and him alone.

Of course, she had doubted he would believe her. What on earth had he done to make her think otherwise?

'Summer—'

'Ask me,' she repeated, her voice raised this time but stronger.

'No.' The word clawed against his throat.

She cocked her head to the side and his heart pounded. He knew where this was going and he wanted to stop it. He wasn't prepared for this.

'Why not?'

'Because I don't have to.' He knew that wouldn't be enough and that she'd be right to demand more. Because he saw it now. She'd had the same look on her face the morning of the argument. 'Because I know.'

'Know what? That if I said it was yours that I'd be telling the truth?'

He nodded, shame, anger, guilt making him nauseous.

'I want to hear you say it,' she said, her voice trembling.

He gritted his teeth. It was the least she deserved and, if he had his way, the first of everything. 'I believe you.'

He cursed mentally, knowing the truth of it. Knowing that the child was his, but more than that—Summer was Kyros's child. She had been telling the truth the day he'd kicked her out of his apartment, treating her no better than a...

He fisted his hands. He didn't want to know, but the question was burning a hole in his empty chest. 'Were you going to tell me?' He couldn't look at her as he asked the question. He didn't want to see what her expressive features betrayed.

But she was hell-bent on making him work for his answer. It was only when he met her gaze that she responded.

'After. When a DNA test would have been safe.' Her eyes told him that she'd wanted to lie, wanted to say never, but she wasn't like that. Why hadn't he seen that then? Why hadn't he believed her?

A phone ringing in the distance cut through the moment. Summer looked behind her and then back to him. 'I have to get that.'

'We will talk about this,' he warned.

'Fine. But... I just... I need to get that.'

She disappeared into the bowels of the building before he could argue and suddenly Theron felt dizzy. He turned, with no idea where he was going, just knowing that he needed to get back outside. The corridors were too dark, the house too damp, empty... It was lifeless and he couldn't breathe. Bursting through a door that led out from the back of the house, he bent over, his hands on his knees, pulling air into his lungs.

Had he missed it? The mole on her collarbone? No. He remembered putting his thumb over it, remembered the strange sense of recognition stirring within him. Something sure and strong tightened in his gut. Kyros had the same mole. He was proud of the strange family trait. Every Agyros had it. Theron remembered it, because once as a teenager Lykos had found him trying to draw one on his clavicle and mocked him mercilessly for it.

Theé mou. How could she be Kyros's daughter? The old man had been faithfully married to his wife—his incredibly sick wife—hadn't he? Theron had never known Kyros to leave her side. He'd never spent a night away from her, never had anything but love in his words and actions towards her.

But Theron had only known him for fifteen years. Perhaps something had happened before that? Summer was, what…early twenties?

Early twenties and pregnant. He tried to cast his mind back to that night. How many times had they made love? How many times had they used protection? That he couldn't quite remember was damning enough. He'd been utterly mindless in his desire for her.

A desire that hadn't been misguided. He'd thought himself a fool for thinking her so pure and so bright that night. But he'd *not* been wrong. He hadn't misread her, been fooled or tricked. Summer was absolutely all of the things he'd thought and wanted that night.

He pulled himself up and tried to fill his lungs with oxygen, but he feared they'd never fill again. He was going to be a father. Something primal, instinctive roared to life within him. A possessive, determined, living need welled inside him with such ferocity it almost scared him.

Was this what his own father had felt? And his mother? Had his birth been planned or, as with him and Summer, had the pregnancy been a shock, a surprise?

He had no one to ask these questions, no one to tell him about his parents, their relationship, their lives, their hardships. Both Kyros and Althaia had tried to help him find someone who was connected to his life, but they hadn't been able to find anyone who had known his parents.

And now he was going to be a parent himself. The vow didn't even form words in his head before he felt it in his heart. His child would *never* have questions about their heritage. His child would never feel the losses that he had experienced. It would never want for a single thing. And instinctively he knew Summer would feel the same. It was there in her determination, her challenge to him.

Ask me.

It had been as much a demand as it had been a test.

One he had already failed.

There was only one possible way forward now.

Summer found him sitting on the old stone steps at the back of the house, shrouded by the night. She'd hung up after talking with Star, who had left Duratra and headed into the desert to find the second half of the key to wherever and whatever held the family's missing diamonds. A part of Summer quivered with fear that Star might not find it, and that she herself might not find this hidden location where her great-

great-great-grandmother had placed the family heir-loom. And without the diamonds they wouldn't meet the terms of their grandfather's will and be able to sell the estate to Lykos, so that they could pay for their mother's treatment.

The other part was trembling because of a certain Greek magnate staring into the sky, looking as if he had no plans to leave.

I believe you.

If he'd said it immediately, freely even, she might not have trusted him. But he'd said it as if it had cost him something and she couldn't understand what that might be.

Kyros was absolutely one hundred per cent committed to his wife and family. I know this to be true. I have seen it with my own eyes.

'What is my father to you?' Summer had been so busy putting the pieces together that she'd spoken before she'd thought. And the look in his eyes when his gaze rose to meet hers made her wish she hadn't.

The tangle of hurt, resentment, love, protection… all these emotions knitted together in his eyes.

'Everything,' he replied, turning back to look up at the stars. 'I still…'

She flinched, knowing that words of disbelief would have finished that sentence.

'I do believe you,' he said, as if he'd felt rather than seen her hurt. 'It's just *hard*. I've known him since I was twelve.'

And I've never known him, she thought as something twisted in her heart.

'He gave me everything that I have today and I would do anything for him.' He said it simply, easily, like floating on water, but she felt the words like a stone, weighing and pressing him down. Maybe he couldn't see it.

'What happened? How…?' He asked as if she held the answer to understanding a shocking mystery.

'I don't know. I was hoping to ask him.'

'And…your mother? What does she say?'

'I can't ask her,' she replied past the hurt in her chest.

'Why not? Surely she'd—'

'She's not well,' Summer said, cutting him off, the stubborn jut to her jaw putting an end to his line of questioning. His eyes softened, and she didn't want to see it. Things had been much easier when he'd been an ocean away and ignorant. She'd hardly thought of him at all.

Liar.

'Does she know about the baby?' he asked quietly as if, without being told, he knew that darkness stalked the fringes of their conversation. Loss. And possibly worse.

'No.'

He nodded once. 'Well, we can stay here until you're ready.'

'Ready for what?' she asked, not quite sure what he was talking about.

'To return to Greece.'

'Why would I return to Greece?'

She couldn't understand why he was looking at her as if she had lost her mind, or memory, or something.

'Because that is where we'll live.'

'What?' she demanded, heat creeping up her neck and twisting in her belly.

'When we're married.'

'What?' she said, louder this time.

Theron's hands were cold and he felt as if he'd swallowed stones. He clenched his jaw, stifling the desperation he felt lest it show in his tone when he next spoke. He was used to people simply doing what he said. Managing his business like an army. It was how he'd achieved what he had in such a short time. Supreme self-confidence and determination. But Summer was like a live wire, twisting and turning, and he never knew what she would do next.

'We will marry,' he announced and this time she laughed.

'No.'

'What do you mean, no?' he demanded, shocked by her response.

'What do you mean, we will marry?'

'Well—' he frowned, confused '—exactly that.'

'Yeah. Me too. So *no*.'

Theron frowned. Opened his mouth. Closed it again. He'd not foreseen this. He stood up, feeling that he needed the height advantage, and regretted it as she seemed intuitively to know he'd done so on purpose. He realised this the moment she took two steps back to meet him at eye level.

'I don't know you,' she growled softly.

'I hardly think that matters,' he replied, mentally batting away how much her statement had hurt.

'Really?' she demanded. 'What *does* matter then?'

'That you have my name and my protection,' he insisted.

'I'm happy with my name, Theron, and I don't need your protection.'

Her response was so damn reasonable, when he felt anything but. He wanted to shout, to yell, to roar against this strange sense of everything he'd never known he'd wanted slowly slipping through his fingers. He tried to get himself under control before he made things worse, but Summer seemed to be one step ahead of him at every turn.

'Look,' she said, striving for a calm that felt impossibly out of reach. 'Clearly we have to talk, but it's late. Why don't you go and come back tomorrow, or...?'

'Never? Would you prefer that?' he demanded, cursing himself and his own anger when he saw her eyes flare in defiance. She made him so...*emotional.* He took a breath. 'I'm not going anywhere,' he explained, keeping his tone as calm as possible.

'You can't stay here,' Summer replied with a shake of her head.

'It's not as if there aren't any free rooms,' he pointed out.

She held his gaze for a moment, an explosion of wicked sparks in her eyes. 'By all means, take your pick.'

She'd known, he realised half an hour later, as he lay down on a dusty mattress that was sure to give him allergies in a room that probably hadn't been heated for one hundred years. She'd done it on purpose, leaving the choice to him, knowing there was literally no good option. This was the sixth room he'd tried and he was too exhausted to care any more.

The wind howled down an empty fireplace and reduced the room's temperature by another degree or two. It was definitely the least he deserved and if there was more, Theron swore to himself and his unborn child, then he'd do whatever it took. Because they were now—whether Summer liked it or not—his family.

CHAPTER FIVE

THERE WAS SOMETHING in the walls. Theron didn't believe in ghosts, yet he would have sworn that he'd heard footsteps. But when he'd stuck his head into the corridor it had been empty. And then, after returning from the most unpleasantly cold shower he'd had in at least ten years, he'd thought there was someone actually in the room, even though it was obviously empty.

He threw his trousers on and rubbed his hair dry with a towel, thinking back over last night. The way he'd reacted, the way he'd demanded she marry him…

An explosion crashed through the estate and adrenaline instantly drenched his body as he ran towards the sound.

'Summer!' His heart pounding, he tried to figure out where the sound had come from, searching left and right. 'Summer!' he yelled again. He cursed in Greek and careened around a corner to find a slowly dissipating cloud of dust. In the middle of it was Summer, dressed in jeans, a jumper stretched over her belly, dust in her hair and on her face, coughing.

'What the hell is going on?' he demanded, striding forward, grasping her arm and pulling her from what looked suspiciously like a giant hole in the wall.

Summer sucked in huge lungfuls of air and shook her head, sending little bits of centuries-old plaster flying. She coughed once more, fanning her watery eyes and then looked up at him, her eyes seeming to clear.

'Are you okay?' she asked.

'Me?'

'Yes. You've gone quite pale,' she stated before marching off, patting down her clothing as she went.

'Stop!' he commanded, regretting it the instant she turned with a raised eyebrow. 'Don't give me that look,' he growled. 'You emerge from a *hole in the wall* as if it were nothing, and I don't have a right to know what's going on?'

'A right? No. You don't have a *right*. But if you would *like* to know, you could change your tone, lower your voice and ask nicely. *That* might work.'

He stared after her for a moment, floored. Althaia had been the one and only woman to put him in his place and he couldn't shake the feeling that she would have definitely been on Summer's side.

'Can we start again?' he called after her.

He could have sworn he heard a huff of laughter.

Summer rested her head against the tiled wall of the shower as water rushed over her head, neck and shoulders. She'd done her best to keep the surprise from her face as Theron had found her emerging from the hole in the wall. She'd been on her way back from searching the last of the secret tunnels in the east wing when she'd caught her shoulder on a bit of protruding battening which had knocked her centre of gravity and she'd fallen against the hole already there from Elias's search and it had collapsed. She'd managed not to fall, but the mess it had created was impressive.

She eased out the kink in that same shoulder as she reviewed her progress. So, the jewels weren't hidden in the east wing's secret passageways. Summer had now thoroughly searched all of them. The ones around the main section of the building appeared to be more functional, serving as shortcuts through the building, which left just the secret passageways in the west wing.

She had the map from Skye, could only hope that Star was close to retrieving the key…but none of it would matter if she couldn't locate where Catherine had hidden the jewels.

But the look in Theron's eyes kept bursting in on her thought processes. Unwanted but determined— just like the man himself. He'd been worried about her—because she hadn't missed that. She couldn't have missed it. It had shone from his—admittedly angry—eyes, but the worry was what had pinned her heart.

He'd stayed last night, which was more than she'd expected of him. He hadn't browbeaten her, ridiculed her or threatened her last night. Not that she'd expected that of him—or at least not what she knew of him from their time in Greece before he'd kicked her out.

She sighed in defeat. She owed him an explanation at least and, in all likelihood, a lot more. But before she could change her mind, she turned off the shower, dressed and went to find him.

He was looking out of the large library window, his profile outlined by morning sun, the rest of him cast in shadow. His profile made her heart soar inexplicably. She hadn't realised how lonely she'd felt in the last few weeks in the estate on her own. But, if she were honest with herself, she'd felt it ever since returning from Greece. There was something about Theron that had made her feel...seen. Briefly, at least.

He turned and for just a moment she felt the burn of his gaze, the power he had to simply light up her body as if she were hackmanite, left to glow in the dark even in his absence. And then he blinked and she shivered.

'It's a long story,' she said, half hoping he'd tell her to skip to the end.

'I have time. And breakfast,' he said, pointing to the table, where fruit, toast and tea were all gathered. Her stomach growled at the sight and she realised she'd forgotten to eat that morning. He smiled wryly, snared an apple before taking a seat.

She sat in the opposite chair, swept her legs up under her and picked at the buttery toast. 'Just before I went to Greece, Mum had been diagnosed with stage three cancer. We were waiting to hear back on the treatment plans.'

'Summer, I... I'm so sorry.'

She nodded, gritting her teeth against the wave of nausea that always came when she thought of her mum's illness. It swept at her ankles and feet, threatening to topple her sense of up and down. But, strangely, Theron's words anchored her. Their sincerity surprised her and touched her. 'Thank you.'

'Is that why you were looking for Kyros?' he asked.

Her stomach churned, making the nausea acidic. She pressed a hand against her sternum to hold it back. 'I didn't…it wasn't like that.' She shook her head, fearful that he believed she was trying to replace one parent with another. 'Kyros wasn't a backup or—'

'Summer.' His tone was firm but gentle. 'That is not what I meant. At all. I know that's not what you were looking for.' The way he said it, the current that swirled beneath his tone, pushed back the ache just enough for her to feel thankful that he didn't think the worst of her. She breathed, but it was full of sadness as she remembered the fresh hurt laid over the rejection of both Theron and her father.

'When I came back from Greece, we found out that the treatment Mum needed couldn't be offered.'

'Why not?'

'Different areas in the UK have different access to certain treatments. We didn't live in the right area for the treatment she needs.' She shook her shoulders free of the tendrils of hurt and fear that still reached for her now. And if she concentrated she could hear the tick-tock of time running out. Every time she thought of her mother, the illness, it prompted a wave of helpless fear that made her need to find the jewels feel like claws scratching at her ankles.

'That's…' the look on Theron's face was incredulous '…barbaric.'

She nodded, agreeing with him completely. 'Just over two months ago, Skye got a call informing us that our grandfather had passed away. We never knew him,' she said quickly, forestalling his sympathy, 'and I don't think I would have wanted to. He clearly wasn't a pleasant man, having cut his daughter from his life and financial support. Still, he left me and my sisters the estate and everything in it—on one condition. That we find the Soames diamonds that have been missing for over one hundred and fifty years. No one searching for them had discovered their hiding place in all that time.'

'But you have?'

'Sort of.' She nodded. 'We uncovered a collection of journals, a photograph and a necklace hidden here in the library. In the journals was a coded message, explaining that our great-great-great-grandmother had hidden the jewels from her undeserving husband after her marriage.'

'In the walls…?'

Summer couldn't help but laugh. She supposed it did sound a little crazy. It was, after all, a one hundred and fifty-year-old treasure hunt. 'The estate suffered some fire damage in the mid to late eighteen-hundreds and was rebuilt by a French architect named Benoit Chalendar.'

Theron frowned. 'As in Chalendar Enterprises?'

'Mm-hmm. He put in a secret recess behind the shelves over there,' she said, pointing behind him. 'And also built secret passageways behind the walls here in the estate for Catherine Soames's amusement. They turned out to be a sanctuary for her. And somewhere within the passageways is a room, or a box, where the diamonds have been kept safely locked away.'

'So, you have the key?'

'I *think* so,' she said, desperately hoping that to be the case. 'Star is in Duratra now and says that she knows where the necklace is.'

'What does a necklace have to do—?'

Summer scrunched her nose, realising she was telling this all wrong. 'Sorry. The necklace we found here in the library interlocks with a necklace that the royal family of Duratra have been protecting. Together, they form the key to where the diamonds are.'

He frowned, as if mostly keeping up. 'So you have a map of the tunnels, the key is nearly here, but you don't know *where* in the passageways the diamonds are locked?'

Summer nodded.

'And you won't inherit the estate if you don't find the diamonds?'

She nodded again.

'But if you find the diamonds, inherit the estate, then you can sell it to Lykos, so that you can…pay for your mother's treatment,' he concluded, understanding finally dawning in his eyes.

'Exactly.'

'Summer, I can give you that money,' Theron insisted.

She bit her lip and shook her head. 'In exchange for?'

'What? No, there would be no strings,' he said. For

a moment he appeared offended that she had thought such a thing. But he'd said it as if he actually believed it.

'Oh, so maybe when we have a disagreement about me having a home birth—'

'A home birth?' he choked.

'Or the name of our child, or where I live with our child, or—'

'We *will* be getting married.'

'Or *whether* we marry... Theron, if I take your money for my mother's treatment it will always be there. We are going to be parents together. We are going to look after a baby, a child, a teenager and a young adult. We *have* to be equals in this. I could not spend the rest of our lives in your debt.'

It was probably the only thing she could say to cut through the fog of his indignation and incomprehension. Because Theron knew the weight of such a debt. He felt it every single day. Even now, thinking of Kyros, he felt the hot ache of guilt. Coming to England had been the first time Theron had ever lied to him. A new client. The words had stuck in his throat when he'd lied to the man who had given him so much that no repayment could ever be compensation enough. Theron should have never kept this—kept *her*—from him.

'I will stand for nothing less, Theron.'

'You shouldn't,' he agreed, swearing to himself that he would never do such a thing to her. The pride he felt seeing her determination, seeing the spark of golden fire in her hazel eyes, was bewitching. In that moment he knew that she would be fierce as a mother, protective, sure and powerful. It humbled him.

And then it scared him. What kind of father would he be if his first act had been to cast out the mother of his child and accuse her of...? His heart pounded in his chest and he clenched his fists, trying to refocus himself as a cold sweat broke out at his neck.

'How long have you been searching the tunnels?' He forced the words out, trying to distract himself.

'Skye sent pictures of the map about a month ago.'

He cursed, his mind moving from himself to her in a heartbeat. 'You've been searching these tunnels on your own for a month?'

'We're all doing our bit,' she said defensively. 'Skye is in France with Benoit—they're figuring out a few things through the engagement and Star is in Duratra trying to get the key back from Sheikh Khalif Al Azhar. And I'm supposed to find the jewels, except I can't.'

She sounded so lost he wanted to help. Needed to.

'How did you find the map and the key?' he asked, genuinely curious.

'There were coded messages in the journal entries we discovered, and the last message said, *You will find them when the map and the key are brought together.* Which is fine, but we don't have the time to wait. If the diamonds are here then I *should* be able to find them. Yet I've been through the passageways and the journals and I can't see where they might be hidden.

Catherine writes so much about faith and love and truth, and *trust*, but...'

'That is not quite your area of expertise? Because you like touching and knowing and understanding?'

She looked up at him as if surprised that he recognised that about her, but then his words incited a different understanding. Her cheeks heated, raising his own temperature, the pulse of desire catching and flashing the entire length of his body.

Mine.

But it was more than desire. It was more than recognising someone as sexually compatible. This time it was primal, animalistic. He'd never felt anything so powerful in his entire life. She was his and carrying his child. The cry of possession, loud, insistent and undeniable, tolled through his entire body.

The fierceness of it scared him. Because already to want that much, to need it...it was spinning out of his control and he was *never* out of control. He'd never been out of control. Before her. He drew in a lungful of air to stop the way the ground seemed to shimmer beneath his feet.

'Let's get out of here,' he said, rising as he spoke, surprising them both. His skin itched and he felt half suffocated by his thoughts and by this estate.

'That wasn't my fault,' Theron growled, wondering how quickly he could book a dental appointment back home. His molars were getting a pounding from the clench of his jaw.

Beside him in the car, Summer slowly exhaled.

'That was most *definitely* your fault. You're too far out in the road.'

'What road? It's little more than a dirt track,' he replied, outraged.

'Do you want me to drive?' she asked, not wholly sarcastically.

Theron actually *felt* the look of utter disbelief on his features and tried to ignore the way she bit her lip to stop herself from smiling.

Following the satnav directions on the postcode he'd plugged in, he tried not to become distracted by the slashes of verdant green stretching along the horizon in ways he'd never seen before. But from the corner of his eye he could see Summer's fingers twisting in her lap.

'I want to apologise.' The words fell from his lips urgently, before he could change his mind.

Summer flicked a confused glance at him. 'What for?'

It was a valid question. There were quite a number of options. He saw her bite her lip just before he returned his eyes to the road.

'The way I…behaved,' he said, the words twisting, hot, guilty and painful, in his gut. 'The way I treated you in Greece.' He shook his head. 'Sorry doesn't change it, but I am very and truly sorry.'

He felt the press of her gaze against his skin, checking the road before turning to look at her, hoping that she saw the truth of his words. But it cost him dearly, because he saw the depth of her hurt from that day. He turned back to the road only after she nodded.

'Where are we going?' Summer asked after a few minutes. 'Only I don't like being away from the estate too long.'

Theron paused for a beat. 'When was the last time you actually left the estate?'

She pressed her lips together and looked out of the window. Clearly she hadn't left. He frowned. From what she had said, they had arrived for the funeral nearly two months ago and her sisters had left nearly one month ago. All that time with nothing but searching for the diamonds to distract her from her worry about her mother.

Waiting for the inevitable, hoping for a miracle.

He knew that feeling well. It had been written on his soul during the days he'd spent with Kyros beside Althaia's bedside in the hospital room as the monitors beeped down to a flat line. Theron had hurt with Kyros, cried with him, paced with him and held both his and Althaia's hands. He'd realised in that hospital room that Kyros and Althaia had been in his life longer than his own parents had. The love he had borne witness to in those weeks, and over the years, had made it so hard for him to believe what Summer had told him in Greece.

How ironic then that as he looked at Summer now he suddenly saw Kyros in her. It wasn't the mole on her collarbone or the shape of her face. It was her eyes. The way that she faced the future with a sense of inevitability. As if braced for hurt.

He remembered that feeling. Waiting for the next blow, emotional or physical, it didn't matter. He'd had to cut himself off from feelings, he'd had to embrace a numbing to live through that and he didn't want Summer to experience that. He wouldn't let that happen.

He turned off the main road and cut down a track, wincing as the car's suspension took a pounding. Perhaps he should have rented a four-wheel drive.

He was focused so hard on the road and the car that he hadn't looked further until he heard Summer gasp. Having grown up in Piraeus, practically on the beach, Theron was faintly dismissive of her reaction to what was presumably a small strip of blue. Until he looked up.

'Oh.'

The car rolled to a stop and they stared out at the incredible stretch of sand and the ribbon of blue bisecting the horizon. It was as if he were looking at an optical illusion. Both far and near, impossibly wide yet completely attainable. It made him feel small, as if he were the tiniest speck of sand in the universe.

Summer got out of the car and he followed, watching her eyes grow round with awe and surprise. 'It's beautiful,' she exclaimed as she pulled her coat around her, walking towards the path to the sea.

The wind whipped across his face as he followed her, drawn to her like the tide was to the land. The pulse of the sea had been like an echo of his heartbeat; it was the most constant thing in his life. To hear the crash of waves on a quiet day brought him peace. The same kind of peace, he realised now, that he'd felt in Summer's company that night back in Greece.

As the pathway opened up to the beach, the stretch

of sand before them was endless. They drew to a stop and unaccountably his fingers found hers, their palms touching and easing the tension in his chest for the first time since the day before. The sun was warm on his face, taking a little of the sting out of the wind's bite, and he closed his eyes for just a moment.

Unbidden, the memory of his mother's laugh came to him on the wind. The press of her lips to his cheek, the warming of his heart, something soft that he couldn't quite place…and then it was gone. He breathed through the hurt, forcing himself forward towards the water. He felt Summer's gaze on his skin and he resisted the urge to reach up and capture it, to hold it there.

'You like the sea,' she observed.

He nodded. 'Lykos and I spent nearly every evening at the beach. We'd sneak out of the orphanage after lights out and just sit there. The sea, the stars… My father was a fisherman and being out there, I felt…' he sighed '…connected, I suppose.' He could feel her silent questions pressing against him and owed her that much at least. 'I was five when they died. The earthquake, it was a six point zero,' he said, shaking his head. 'Devastating. It killed over one hundred and forty people and injured thousands.' He no longer saw the sea, the English horizon.

The sound of the tide became a roar, a rumble, the shift of the sand beneath his feet became a tremor. His heartbeat pounded in his ears. In his mind he put his arm out to the doorframe to brace himself. He was screaming for his mother, for his father. They were on the other side of the house. He was all alone and tears were blurring his vision, the whole room was shaking. Where were his parents? Then he saw him—his father, he was coming to get him, his mother following just behind. They were coming for him and they would all be okay. He wouldn't be alone and…

Theron clenched his jaw against the hot press of tears against the backs of his eyes, refusing to let them fall. He focused on the sound of the waves, their gentle sweep across the sand somehow making it easier for him to speak the hurt of his past, as if it took his words and brought them back changed. 'A ceiling beam came down on top of my father and caught my mother. She died later in hospital.'

'Theron—'

He squeezed Summer's hand gently. He knew. He felt her sympathy. 'I was taken to an orphanage. Neither of my parents had family, so that was where I ended up. And where I met Lykos,' Theron said, shaking his head, unable to help the smile pulling at his lips. 'He was… I had lost my family, but I found a brother,' he said, realising just how hard the last ten years had been without him. Even though it still felt as if Lykos was in his head sometimes.

'But when I met him in Greece you seemed more like business acquaintances.'

'We had a falling out,' Theron stated.

'Did it have something to do with my father?' she asked.

Theron kept his features neutral, even though the mention of her father still twisted a knife. Theron should have called Kyros last night. He was torn between loyalty to the man who had been like a father to him and the woman who carried his child.

'Yes,' he said, finally answering her question about Lykos but reluctant to delve into it further.

'How did you meet Kyros?' Summer asked, as if sensing he wasn't going to say any more.

'He found us running scams on the streets. We were picking pockets, raising hell, the usual wayward stuff,' he said, a smile pulling at his lips. They were some of the best memories he had. 'Lykos had picked his pocket, but when he saw the photo in it he said we had to give it back.

'The photo was of him and his wife dancing.' It was only later, when Theron had met Althaia and realised how badly the multiple sclerosis had ravaged her body, that he'd realised the significance of the photo. Kyros eventually told him it was the last time they had danced. 'He wanted to reward us for returning it to him. Lykos,' he said, smiling broadly at the memory of the then fifteen-year-old's audacity, 'demanded one hundred euros. Kyros laughed, insisted that he wanted to give us something much more valuable than that.

'He paid for our education at one of the most exclusive schools in Athens and promised us that if we graduated then we would come and work with him.'

Theron looked out at the endless sea, marvelling at what an incredible gift they'd been given—the opportunity to be more than a statistic, a failure. They hadn't been stupid, even then he and Lykos had known. Life half on the streets, half in the orphanage, little education or hope even after that…it didn't paint a pretty picture. For all that life had been fun with Lykos, it also had nights full of terror, days full of worry—where was the next beating going to come from, where was the next meal…? Life hadn't existed past that.

'We stayed at the orphanage, but went to a good school. It was a little rough at the beginning—a few kids trying it on—but Lykos put a stop to that immediately. It helped that he was a couple of years older and a hell of a lot bigger. Kyros putting us in that school got us off the streets, gave us an education we would never have had. On Sundays we'd go round to Kyros's house for dinner. He'd ask us what we were learning, how our week had been, and he'd tell us about his business. We didn't realise, but even then he was preparing us to work for him.'

'And Althaia?'

Theron looked at Summer. Her hazel eyes had dimmed, the green clearer in them than ever. She'd lost some of the colour he liked seeing so much in her cheeks and for the first time he wondered how Summer would have felt about the woman her father had chosen to be with.

CHAPTER SIX

'SHE JOINED US on the days when she could. Which wasn't often,' Theron said, squinting in the bright sunshine piercing the blue-grey sky that seemed to blanket everything. 'The form of MS she had affects a small amount of people, but the symptoms were difficult and devastating. She was bed-bound for the last two years of her life and constantly battling infections and the slow deterioration of her body.'

Summer's heart hurt for them all and what they'd been through. 'What was she like?' she asked, half wanting to know, half not.

'She was...loving, kind.' He shrugged. 'As interested in us as Kyros was, but often distracted and in pain. Her diagnosis was progressive and it made things very hard for her. Hard for them both.'

Summer wondered if that was why Kyros had strayed—to have one moment outside of the impossible heartbreak he faced. She wondered whether her mother had known, and couldn't quite work out how she felt about it, hating the idea that one thing in her mother's past could change the way Summer saw her. She shook her head, her heart hurting.

'So you both went to work for Kyros when you finished school?' she asked, half changing the subject.

'Yes. For a while.'

Summer frowned, sensing his hesitancy but not the reason why.

Theron took a breath. 'Lykos was two years older than me, so he had gone to work for Kyros before I joined the company. But when I was eighteen, Lykos turned up and told me he was leaving.'

'Why?' she asked.

'I don't know.' Summer didn't know whether he'd realised his hand had tightened around hers, but she soothed her thumb over the back of his hand and his grip loosened. 'He never told me. We had an argument and…we have only spoken once since that day.'

His jaw was clenched so hard that Summer could see the flare of his muscle. She thought he was done, but he surprised her by carrying on.

'He wouldn't tell me why he was leaving, but he wanted me to go with him. I said that we couldn't. That we'd promised to work with him after school. Lykos accused me of choosing Kyros over him and… I couldn't deny it.'

He turned to her, his eyes filled with hurt and pain, warring with that decision all over again.

'I remember every word he said. "It's not real, you know. This little family you've created in your mind from Sunday dinners with Kyros and Althaia. You'll never be part of their real family. You'll be the dog that they feed scraps to for the rest of your life. Because you'll never find a way to repay that debt of yours, will you? *I'm* your family, not them. Come with me".'

'I'm sure he didn't mean it,' Summer said.

'He did,' Theron said, looking out at the sea, the stoicism in his expression heartbreaking for her to see. 'But all I knew was that I had somewhere I felt safe. Somewhere I felt I belonged.' He turned to Summer and she knew, even if he didn't say it. With Kyros he'd found a home. A family. 'I owe Kyros my life. I know what happened to some of the boys at the orphanage. I know what some of them did, what they had to do and where they ended up because of it.'

He lifted the veil holding back his feelings then and she could see it. See it all. The honesty, the fear that it could have been him, the dread of truly horrible things that she could barely conceive of. She might not have had Kyros in her life, but she'd had her mother, her sisters, a roof over her head and a sense of constant security. She understood the awfulness of his childhood, the shock of losing his parents, of being placed in an orphanage—and then being presented with what Kyros was offering. She could see so clearly how impossible it would have been for Theron to have left with Lykos.

'My debt to him will never be repaid.'

Something inside her curled in on itself, as if it recognised something final, something horribly conclusive. She pushed past it to try to see what he wanted her to see.

'Is that why you sent me away in Greece? Because you were trying to pay your debt?' she asked.

'I am in charge of his security. Summer, you're not the first person to claim to be the illegitimate child of a very rich man.'

'He looked right at me—'

'Summer—' he said, as if about to defend him.

'He looked at me and saw nothing.' The words hurt as they poured out of her, her throat thickening with pain.

Theron took a breath. 'He doesn't know about you,' he said simply, with horrifying ease. 'He's not looking for you in young women around him because he doesn't *know* to look. If you were to take a DNA test you could prove it to him. It's a mouth swab. It won't hurt the baby.'

'But it could hurt *me*!' she cried, remembering the pain she'd felt when he'd dismissed her with a glance. *Or you*, she thought, already beginning to see how precarious his position was with Kyros. If she proved herself to be Kyros's child, she couldn't see how that could be any kind of good for Theron. Not with how things stood.

That thought, that realisation, made her frown. 'Is that why you proposed?' Nausea swirled in her stomach.

'Is what why I proposed?'

'Because I'm his daughter. Because—' she shook her head '—I can't imagine how getting your mentor's illegitimate daughter pregnant with an illegitimate child would go down particularly well.'

'I proposed because family is everything. I learned that from him. I cannot allow you to have our child, unmarried.'

'My mother was unmarried when she had me, so don't you dare—'

He held his hands up in surrender.

She shook her head in disgust. 'Kyros might have taught you about family, but my mother taught me about love. And love isn't a debt you can repay.' Her heart ached, her soul felt heavy and her tongue thick with grief. 'Don't ask me again to marry you,' she ordered, before storming off down the beach.

He'd felt it. For just a moment, the softening between them. He'd hardly dared to ease into it, a softness that felt both strange but familiar. Like a half-forgotten song. Until she'd asked why he'd proposed.

Love isn't a debt you can repay.

Her words had echoed in the silence of the journey back to the estate and it felt as if they were eroding his foundations—the very things that he'd clung to for security for all these years. He searched his heart and had to admit the truth. There had been a part of him that sought to appease a future he could see on the horizon. A reckoning with Kyros that he'd perhaps always sensed coming in one form or another.

But it wasn't the only truth. And that was the thing that scared him the most.

After their return he had spent a couple of hours in the room he'd taken as his, answering work emails, concluding business with one client and reassuring another, before going to look for Summer.

As he rounded the corner to the kitchen, she was drawing various ingredients from the fridge that he registered with disgust.

'What is that?' he demanded.

'Dinner.'

'It is no such thing,' he replied, taking steps towards the monstrous selection of food she had gathered together. She turned on him, and had to lean back to peer up at him. He hadn't intended to get so close that he could smell the faint traces of salt and sea air still clinging to her clothes and skin. But he wouldn't retreat. Couldn't.

'There is nothing wrong with a cheese sandwich,' she said defiantly.

'"Dinner" is supposed to be *hot*. And it should most definitely have a vegetable in there somewhere.'

'Fine. Cheese and tomato then,' she snarked. Only he wished she hadn't, because the gold flecks in her eyes sparkled and danced when she did.

'Tomatoes are a fruit,' he dismissed. She had to step back as he went to the fridge to see what there was and sighed heavily. 'Is this an English thing?' he demanded.

'What?'

'A horrible relationship with food.'

'No. It's just that…well…' He turned to find her looking uncomfortably at the floor and he bit his tongue. He hadn't meant to shame her. 'Skye cooked.

For us,' she clarified, 'when we were growing up. She always cooked.'

'Mariam can't cook?' he asked, more gently this time.

'She can. Actually, she's a great cook,' Summer said, her shoulders tensing slightly at the mention of her mother. 'It's just that…she was a bit scatty when it came to mealtimes. She'd always be lost in a sunset, or her yoga or…like, right now, she's focused on her candle magic and…' She trailed off and Theron hoped to God the confusion he felt wasn't on his face this time.

'You've done it again.'

'Done what?' she asked.

'You've stopped mid-sentence.'

'Oh, well, I was expecting some kind of commentary on candle magic.'

Theron frowned. It might not be his thing, but who was he to judge? Althaia had insisted on reading his coffee grains whenever he had visited on a Sunday morning. 'Nope. I don't have any. But I'm curious how you and science fit with such a free spirit.'

'Not easily,' Summer said, and he wondered if she was aware of the tension in her voice. 'I sometimes felt too serious for her, but I always felt loved.'

He doubted that she realised how much she defended her mother to him. As if it was important to her that he thought well of Mariam. He gestured for her to take a seat as he finally figured out what he could do with the limited ingredients in the fridge, pulling the potatoes out before he went looking for a pan.

'You cook?' she asked.

'Yes,' he stated.

'I thought you'd be more of a restaurant kind of guy,' she said, shrugging.

He smirked. 'I do that too, but...' He sighed. 'Althaia taught me. On Sundays, when we'd visit, she'd teach me a new recipe and we'd eat it together. *Not like that*,' he echoed, his hand coming down in the air in a cutting movement. *'Like this,'* he said, smiling as he repeated the gesture at Althaia's 'correct' angle. But then he remembered the days she hadn't been able to help so much. She'd sat in the corner of the kitchen, rattling off directions like an army general.

'I'm sorry,' Summer said, and he frowned. 'She clearly meant a lot to you.'

He nodded and poured boiling water over the potatoes and then pulled flour down from the shelf.

'What are we having?' she asked, eyeing the potatoes and flour suspiciously.

'Gnocchi.'

'Really?' she asked incredulously. 'You're just *whipping up* some *gnocchi*?'

'Yes,' he replied, and a touch of pride flashed through him as the gold in her eyes sparkled.

He opened his mouth to ask the question that had snared in his mind earlier, but he hesitated, reluctant to broach it. And he wouldn't have if he hadn't thought that Summer needed it. Her mother was important to her and, whatever was holding her back, she would never forgive herself if anything happened while she held onto that hurt.

'Why are you angry with her?' he asked gently.

'Who?'

'Your mother.'

'I'm not.'

Theron just managed to stop himself from contradicting her, choosing instead to wait her out.

Summer pressed her lips together and stared at her hands until her shoulders sagged ever so slightly.

'She told me she didn't know who my father was.'

Summer watched as he filled the pan with water and put it on the lit stove. He was waiting for more, she recognised that in him now. Waiting for her to say what she needed. She liked that about him. It would make him a good father, she realised with a jolt that hurt her heart a little as she realised just how much she'd missed.

'Mum told me that they'd met, that the time they'd shared had been magical, but that they hadn't exchanged names, so she'd never been able to tell him about me. Over the years there might be slight variations, a few extra details, or some that changed. But it had always been an almost mystical holiday romance. As if it had been outside of time and incredibly special, but entirely contained within that bubble.

'But that was a lie. She could have reached out to him. Even if Kyros was married, even if it was difficult, even if he'd said he didn't want anything to do with me,' she said, the words rushing out on a shaky breath, 'I would have preferred that to...'

'To?' he nudged gently.

'To growing up searching every face, every person,

for the thing that I felt I was missing. Not knowing, it was a physical pain for me. An ache for something I couldn't even name.'

A sense of security—was that what a father gave? Summer wondered. A template for how men should behave, how they should treat her as a woman? Was *that* what she'd missed? A safe haven, somewhere to turn, no matter how hard or bad or difficult things got? She loved her mother fiercely and with her whole heart, but keeping her father from her had hurt her and shaped her in ways Mariam could never have realised.

And in that moment, in that half breath between that thought and her next, she realised something that would change her life irrevocably. She could never do that to her child. No matter what happened between her and Theron, no matter what, her child would know their father. They would be a part of each other's lives if she had to move heaven and earth to make it happen.

She looked up and blinked back a shimmer of tears as Theron's gaze searched hers as if he wondered where her thoughts had taken her. She shook thoughts of her child from her head, memories of her own childhood in her heart. Now wasn't the time for that conversation with Theron. There was so much more to speak of first. She bit her lip and looked out of the kitchen window at the night sky beyond.

'So yes, absolutely, growing up without a father hurt. But it was a hurt that I had made peace with. Until I found the photo.'

Theron put down the pan and walked to where she sat.

'Before then, it wasn't anyone's fault. It was a horrible *absence*. But finding the photo… She'd lied to me and I can't even tell her that I know. She betrayed me and I have so much… I'm so *angry*.'

He reached her on the first sob of breath and pulled her out of the chair on the second. 'Oh, God,' she half cried. 'What if we don't find the diamonds? What if Mum doesn't get the treatment and what if I am still angry with her when she…?'

She couldn't bring herself to even say the words.

Theron held out his hand. 'I'd like to show you something.'

Summer followed Theron as he led her down a hallway and through a door to the garden that had become devastatingly overgrown. In a strange way it reminded her of the roses around Sleeping Beauty's castle.

The evening air was surprisingly warm and the sky was a blanket of stars, shockingly bright and clear. The sight of it burned away some of her anger, but not enough. She could still feel it roiling, barely a millimetre beneath the surface. She hated it. She wasn't this person. She was practical, not emotional. Logical, not irrational. But ever since her mother's diagnosis, ever since the discovery of her father's identity, ever since *Theron*, she'd been behaving completely out of character.

She inhaled the scent of honeysuckle and frowned. She'd not seen the beautiful fragrant plant out here. In the dark, Theron seemed to be looking around.

'Neighbours are quite far away?'

'Yes. Why?' she asked, very confused now.

'Good. No one will hear you.'

'You get how that sounds, right?' she asked, unsure whether to laugh or back away.

He looked at her in all seriousness and then a smile broke out across his face, lighting his eyes and making him look his age for the first time since she'd met him. 'Yes. That's the point. You are going to scream.'

'Okay, enough with the psycho talk,' she said, turning back, before he caught her arm to stop her.

'No. I'm serious. All this anger. You're going to scream it out.'

Summer stared up at him, finally understanding what he wanted. 'I don't think—'

Theron sighed. 'That's the point. You *do* think. You think far too much. Screaming? It's visceral, it comes from here,' he said, pressing his hand to her diaphragm, just above the round of her stomach. There was a slight pause, a flare in his eyes, before he masked it. 'You need to let it out because it's damaging. So, scream.'

Summer was so tempted. She could imagine it. How it might feel to release all the emotions bottled up inside her. But she was embarrassed. She'd sound stupid, she'd probably get it wrong, and she'd look—

Every thought stopped as a thunderous bellow cut through the night sky. She turned to Theron, eyes wide and shocked.

'That's how you do it. Your turn.'

She frowned, still unsure.

'Hold on,' he said, placing his hands over his ears

as if he understood her concern, as silly as it might be. 'Go.'

She huffed out a laugh, but he didn't move, just waited for her to get on and do it. Finally, she took a deep breath, looked out across the mass of brambles and stars...and *screamed*.

She winced through the first awkward second or two, but then it rushed out of her, gaining power and volume just at the end.

'*Nai*. Good. Again,' Theron commanded.

Her heart pounding and the pressure in her head and chest beginning to flow, she screamed again, the sound, the anger, the tension, the constant fear she'd been holding in, all purged from her body in one long howl. She nearly choked when she heard Theron join her.

Her blood fizzed in her veins and there was a lightness in her chest that she hadn't felt since Greece. 'People are going to think we're crazy,' she said, laughing.

'That's okay.'

She looked up at him, outlined by the stars in the night sky, his eyes blazing more fiercely than the moon. And then she remembered. That night on the beach. She'd tried to force it from her mind because of the intensity of the feelings, the emotions it brought. Her fingers itched to reach up and brush the stray lock of hair that had fallen across his brow.

Because she wanted to see him. All of him. She wanted so damn much. But she was scared. And that was why she turned back to look out across the garden.

'Was it Lykos who taught you that?'

There was a beat of silence before he answered.

'No. It was Kyros.'

And suddenly it hurt. Hurt that her father had given him this…*thing*, had spent years with Theron, while she'd had nothing. It made her feel mean and angry all over again. But most of all it made her sad.

Once again, he stopped her before she could turn to leave. His hand was at her wrist, a gentle clasp that she could have easily broken, but didn't. Couldn't because of the way she felt alive beneath his touch.

'I remember a similar feeling,' he said, his voice quiet but breathing sincere emotion into the night air between them, 'to the one you described. That anger. At the world, at my parents for dying, at Lykos for leaving. It's as familiar to me as the blood in my veins. And if Kyros hadn't intervened, things might have been very different. But he did.

'Do you think it's possible,' he asked, looking down at her, as if trying to read the eyes she kept hidden from his gaze, 'that Kyros taught me, all those years ago, so that I might be here with you now, showing you?'

The idea behind his words, the intent, was all too much. She felt like a raw nerve, exposed and vulnerable, and she wanted to feel powerful. She wanted to feel confident—all the things she had embraced the night she'd spent with him in Greece. And, before she could stop herself, she reached for him, her hands threaded through his hair, clasped at his neck, pulling him down towards her, and when his lips finally met hers it was as if she could breathe again for the first time.

For just a moment he didn't move and she thought he would pull back, feared that he would leave her breathless and wanting. And then he groaned helplessly against her lips as he deepened the kiss, thrusting his tongue into her mouth at the same time as pulling her against his body and everything in her exploded. Open kisses, tangled tongues and pounding heartbeats were all Summer knew for blissful endless moments that rolled into each other.

She breathed in the scent of him, salt from the sea mixing with honeysuckle and cedar. His hand settled between her shoulder blades and the other swept up her side, perilously close to her breast, but not close enough. Her nipples tightened in anticipation, in need and then—

The harsh, bright ring of the doorbell cut through the night.

Theron reared back, dark slashes of crimson on his cheeks, matching—she was sure—those on her own, his hungry gaze consuming hers until the doorbell rang again and he stepped back. Summer hugged her arms around her body, pulling the edges of her shawl around her shoulders before turning away from the look of…what, regret? Frustration? She didn't want to know.

Hurrying down the corridors, she called that she was coming to whoever it could be at the door at this time of night. The doorbell rang again, spiking her adrenaline for some reason, the urgency of it scratching against her delicate nerves.

She pulled open the door, the heat she felt from Theron hovering in the dark corridor behind her giving her a sense of safety.

A small, bespectacled man stood blinking up at her, frowning as if she were not what he'd expected. Behind him was a long sleek town car with three dark-suited men who, at the sight of Theron looming behind her, came to stand tall, puffing out their chests as if to meet power with power.

She refocused on the man in front of her.

'Ms Summer Soames?'

'Yes.'

'Can I see some identification?'

'Why?'

He inhaled, as if frustrated by her response. 'What I have is—I've been told—of great importance to you and your family and I will not give it into the wrong hands,' he said, his voice imperious. 'It is from Ms Star Soames. I have brought it all the way, in person, from—'

'Duratra! It's the necklace!' Summer cried, making the bespectacled man wince, the suited men around the car start, and Theron draw one step closer. 'Don't go anywhere! Don't move! Theron, please make sure—'

'They don't leave. Got it,' he said as she disappeared into the bowels of the house to retrieve her wallet.

She ran, the whole time her pulse racing, but never as wildly as it had when Theron had kissed her.

It was the key. It was here. Finally.

So why did her thoughts keep veering back to the kiss? Why did she stop in the middle of the corridor to bite her lip where his lips had touched, to try and hold that sense of him to her, instead of rushing to retrieve her identification? Her breath juddered in her chest and she put her hand half out to steady herself. But then she steeled her spine.

It was the key. It was here and she needed it. Now.

She returned to the front of the house with her passport and showed it to the man, who bowed low and when he righted himself presented her with a package as solemnly as if it were a crown jewel.

The man eyed Theron suspiciously, then snapped his fingers and he and the suited men disappeared into the car, which turned in a slow arc before grinding down the gravel path away from the estate.

Last night...

Lykos howled with laughter. 'I still can't believe you took a convertible to Norfolk. Even *I'm* not that ridiculous.'

'The English can't drive. It was not my fault.'

'You keep telling yourself that,' Lykos said with a smirk on his lips. 'Drink up.'

Theron took the last mouthful of his whisky and pulled on his jacket as Lykos palmed an obscene number of notes off to a very happy-looking waitress. As he shrugged into the sleeves of his coat, he could have sworn he still smelt the salt of the North Sea.

'You remembered it wrong, by the way. *You* saw the photo and forced me to agree that we should give it back,' Lykos stated as they stepped out of Victoriana onto the wet pavement, throwing his collar up against the rain, ignoring the man with an umbrella and stalking towards the sleek town car waiting for them.

Theron stood on the steps, staring not at Lykos, holding the door open for him, or the black cabs and yellow lights of London, but the way Summer had run off into the house after receiving the package from Duratra, her focus so all-consuming.

'Look, get in the car, don't get in the car. Not my concern. Whatever you're going to do, do it,' Lykos said, sliding into the back of the car, leaving the door open.

He got in and closed the door, turning to Lykos, scanning his phone for something.

'There's nothing wrong with my memory,' Theron said.

'I ought to sue you for misrepresentation.'

Theron waved him off. After a while he couldn't help himself. 'What are you doing?'

'Looking for that *gnocchi* recipe,' Lykos answered, eyes still glued to the screen. 'Since you clearly turned into a domestic goddess—'

Theron reached for the nearest thing, which happened to be a rather creased newspaper, and threw it at him.

Lykos caught it without looking up, a smirk across his lips.

As they made their way through the city at night, the faint glow of Lykos's screen illuminating the back of the car, Theron spared a brief thought for what Lykos had been doing all these years. Because of his job, Theron had access to as much information on people as he'd ever want. But he'd never looked Lykos up.

'Okay, fine,' his old friend said, putting away his phone just as they pulled to a stop. 'Right, I've got it. Maps, secret passageways, hidden jewels, treasure hunt. Blah, blah, blah.'

'I'm beginning to think you're more interested in me and Summer.'

'No idea what you're talking about,' Lykos hotly denied. 'My only interest is in whether I can get my hands on that castle or not.'

'It's an *estate*,' Theron growled, getting out of the car and staring up at the building it had pulled up in front of. He frowned. He had expected to find Lykos staying in some sleek and impossibly expensive penthouse. And while this definitely ticked the impossibly expensive box, the Regency terrace in a tree-lined road in the heart of Knightsbridge was altogether something *other*. He looked from the house to Lykos and back to the house again as his old friend passed through the wrought iron gate, pressed his thumb against an electronic keypad and pushed open the front door.

'But it *was* the necklace from Duratra, right?' Lykos asked, not bothering to look back as he stalked into the living area, tossed his suit jacket on a chair and went straight to a drinks cabinet to pour himself a whisky. Belatedly, he turned, gesturing to Theron, who nodded and accepted the glass Lykos then gave him.

'Yes, it was the necklace.'

CHAPTER SEVEN

Three days ago...

THERON PACED THE tiled floor of the kitchen.

That kiss.

It had been just like the one on the beach in Piraeus. It had knocked him off his feet and made him lose his mind. Only it hadn't been enough. Not nearly enough. He knew *exactly* what would have happened if they hadn't been interrupted. His body did too and was still clamouring for it. Needy for it.

He shook his head in swift denial of his thoughts and his body. He needed to get a grip and put it to the back of his mind. Summer and her sisters had been searching for the jewels non-stop for nearly two whole months. Dancing to the tune of some now dead relative in order to save their mother. She now had within her grasp the ability to help save her mother's life.

What would he have done for such a chance?

Anything. The answer was swift and sure.

He could see in an instant how nothing would be conceivable for Summer until she found the diamonds.

No thinking about the future, no decision, nothing. Her mother's health and her and her sisters' ability to secure it would have, and clearly had, eclipsed all else.

But there would come a time when they would have to sit down and talk—about their future, their child's future and what that would look like. And before they could do that he needed to know what *he* thought, what *he* wanted it to be.

His mind flashed back, not to Sunday dinners with Kyros and Althaia, not laughing with Lykos on the beach, terrorising tourists and local vendors for money and food, but to sitting in his mother's lap in a room he could barely remember, hands clasped around her neck, cheek to chest, feeling nothing but safe, nothing but love.

That was home. That was what a parent gave a child—what *he* wanted to give *his* child.

But could he give that to Summer?

The sound of water bubbling over the edge of the pan drew him back to the *gnocchi*. Seeing that they were ready, he tossed the potato dumplings into the frying pan with the sauce and finished with salt and pepper, before dividing them between two plates. He found a tray from somewhere and put the plates, some water and cutlery onto the tray and took a deep breath before heading to the library.

As he'd expected, Theron found Summer hunched over the small table where she'd gathered all the journals, her hand resting on the necklace's velvet pouch while the index finger of her other hand traced the handwritten instalments in leather-bound journals that looked exactly what they were: decades old.

He turned on the overhead light, causing Summer to momentarily sit up, blink, and then go back to the journals. Her concentration was fierce and impressive—it must be, to study what she did, to think the way she did—but he worried about the toll it took on her. He placed the food on the table beside her and took his to the chair by the fire.

Over the next few hours Theron came and went and Summer barely moved. He took away the plates, washed up, added logs to the fire, looked at the rows of books on the shelves, but none of the titles caught his eye.

He frowned, looking over at one of the journals Summer had discarded and snagged it from the table without her noticing. Gently, delicately, he fingered the pages, frowning at the tightly curled cursive handwriting, passing dates that spanned months through the late eighteen-hundreds. Unable to resist, he turned to the final page.

I have heard it said that life is lived forwards, yet only to be understood backwards. I believe I know a little of that.

Theron recognised the Kierkegaard quote as one of his favourites, marvelling at how forward-thinking Catherine had been. And then he smiled, realising that he shouldn't be surprised. The Soames women were impressive, and his heart warmed with the hope that their child might be a girl to carry on those same indomitable traits.

Finally, he turned back to Summer, just to watch her. She had fallen asleep, her arm folded beneath her head and her hair falling free, the flames from the fire flickering over the golden rope-like twists. She made his heart expand. He couldn't understand it. Couldn't explain it. But she did.

He stood, rolled his shoulders. Everything was about to change. And he needed to change with it or risk losing everything. He walked over to the table, reluctant to wake her. Beyond the curve of her neck, he could see the map of the estate with the details of the secret passageways that ran just behind the hallways.

The map itself was a thing of beauty. Over one hundred and fifty years old, the detail was incredible. A filigree border surrounded the map and in the light of the fire it looked as if there were two pale gold lines leading down towards the map of the estate, but they stopped just before there was a sense of where they might lead. He peered over Summer's shoulder at the necklace. It was a strange design with two chains. He'd never seen anything like it. He remembered Summer telling him how the two necklaces would fit together to form a key, but it was still a beautiful piece of jewellery.

Then another set of faint gold lines caught his eye and he traced them with his fingertips and smiled. If he were to place the necklace chains along the four gold starter lines, then the pendant would come to rest in the north-west of the estate. He smiled to himself, feeling a deep satisfaction, which he tempered. Whether he had just found the location of the diamonds or not, Summer needed to rest. They would not disappear by the morning.

'Summer?' he whispered gently. He rubbed her shoulder, not wanting to disturb her too much. She shifted in her seat, the hold of sleep strong, and he gently pulled out the chair. Reaching down, he placed an arm beneath her legs and lifted her into his arms. Her eyes fluttered briefly but closed immediately and she leaned against his chest trustingly.

For a moment he stood in the library, Summer in his arms, and felt humbled. And then he turned into the corridors that would take him towards her room and, pushing open the door with his foot, walked to her bed and placed her gently onto the mattress. But as he went to stand, he noticed she had fisted his shirt in her hand. He tried to loosen her fingers, but instinctively he knew that she would wake. And then she'd probably yell at him for taking her away from her search for the diamonds. To avoid such a thing, he toed off his shoes and lay beside her on the bed.

As if sensing his capitulation, she crept closer and pressed into his side. The fine material of his shirt and the thick material of her cardigan were not enough to stop him from feeling the press of her chest against his side, the heat of her body and the scent of cinnamon and spice that he wanted to drown in. He took swift and harsh control of his body before it could spin out of control. He didn't care how much his body wanted or needed, *craved* hers, Summer needed sleep. And it

PIPPA ROSCOE   137

was then that he felt it, stronger than anything he'd felt with Kyros. The bone-deep knowledge that he would protect Summer from anything and everything.

Summer opened her eyes, her fist clenched around an invisible tether she'd felt all through her dreams. It had been like an anchor to something safe, something secure, and she didn't think she'd ever felt peace like it. She opened her hand and smoothed the sheets next to her, frowning slightly at the indentation but deciding that she must have turned in her sleep.

She looked at the clock and started. Nine a.m.! It was *nine*! Suddenly yesterday came crashing through her memories like strobe lighting but all jumbled out of order. The kiss, the beach, the necklace, the library.

Her heart pounded in her chest, her mind torn between the kiss and the necklace.

Necklace first, she decided and threw off the covers, surprised to find herself still in yesterday's clothes.

Swinging her legs over the side of the bed, she shrugged out of the cardigan, pulled her T-shirt over her head. Shower now? Shower later? If she was going into the secret passageways she might as well shower later, she decided, standing up and tugging at the clasp of her bra at her back.

She yelped as Theron rounded the corner and she grabbed the blanket, covering herself as he stepped into the room, frowning at her as if she were behaving strangely.

'I brought you...' Theron trailed off as he stared at her beneath a very furrowed brow. She was behaving like a child, she knew it, but she was practically top-less. 'You know I have seen you naked before, right?' he asked, as if trying to keep a laugh from escaping.

'That was before.'

'Before?'

'Before...*everything*,' she said, unable to quite express the magnitude of *beforeness* that had changed since they'd spent that life-changing night together.

'Right,' he said, as if it were normal for her to be so inarticulate. 'So, I brought you breakfast and—'

'Okay, you can leave it there. And go,' she said, inching her shoulders beneath the blanket and closing her eyes against the state of her room. It was a mess. She'd never had a man in her room before—even if it wasn't technically *her* room but simply the room she was staying in—and there Theron was, and she was so embarrassed.

Why wouldn't he just leave?

'Actually,' he tried again, 'I—'

'Theron, *please*?'

'Please what?' he asked, unable to hide a laugh of incredulity. 'I have brought you breakfast and I have something important to tell you and you act like I'm beneath consideration or...or...' He trailed off, struggling to find the word.

'I've never had a man in my room before, okay? And it's weird. The room's a mess, and I'm embarrassed, and I don't even remember how I got here last night, and—'

'Summer? Breathe.' He locked his eyes onto hers, as if specifically *not* looking around her room, and she did as he asked. Breathed. 'Here is some break-fast. I want you to eat it before I show you something.'

'Can I get changed first?' She thought she saw the ghost of a smile curl the edges of his lips, but he nod-ded so she couldn't see it. She waited, but he stayed there. 'Turn around?' she asked.

'Really?'

'Yes!'

He laughed again, but did as she asked and turned around. She waited a second, as if he might still turn back and catch her in her underwear, but he didn't so she dropped the blanket and grabbed for her clothes. She was being silly because he'd certainly seen more of her the night they'd spent together in Greece. But she felt different now. Her body was different. She reached the wardrobe and grabbed a pair of trousers that she wouldn't mind getting dirty and a shirt so old it felt like silk on her skin. It was cream and pretty and she loved it.

Theron was whispering but she couldn't make out the words.

'What was that?' she asked, slipping her hands through the arms of the shirt.

'You don't want to know.'

'I do, or I wouldn't have asked,' she corrected.

'I said, "Please no more grey…please no more grey".'

Summer pulled up short. 'No more grey?' she re-peated.

Theron turned and she sent him a glare, but not be-fore she saw his eyes snag on the yellow dress hanging in the wardrobe, next to a vivid green one from the same shop. A look of deep longing passed over his features. It was so strong Summer blushed, as memories of the dress, how he had taken it from her body, what he had done to her crashed through the mental barriers she'd placed around that night.

'You shouldn't wear any more grey. Or black.' He shook his head, as if awkward. 'You should always dress in colour,' he said, nodding to the two dresses in the wardrobe. 'I'll be in the library.'

With that he turned on his heel and disappeared, all trace of his gentle laughter gone.

Biting her lip, Summer made her way into the library after eating the toast he'd brought her. Okay, one piece, but it counted, she told herself. She wasn't quite sure what to make of what he'd said about her clothes. If she was honest with herself, she knew they needed to have a proper conversation about exactly what kind of relationship they had and would have in the future. But all that could wait. The diamonds—her mother's health? That *couldn't*.

He was leaning over the table she had sat at last night, studying the map, and she had a sudden image, half memory, half wish, of him behind her, the heat of his skin against hers, as if they had been cheek to cheek. Unconsciously, she raised her hand to her face and he looked up, something passing across his gaze, making her drop her hand. His eyes went to the scarf, back to her face and down to the map without a word.

Awkwardness. She hadn't felt it before…before the kiss.

'So you've searched the east wing and you don't think it's in the central secret passageways?' he asked, still not looking at her.

'Yes. But, even so, there must be one final clue to the precise location because the secret passageways stretch for miles.'

'Well, I think you're right. And I think I know what it is.'

'What?' she demanded, rushing to the table, staring at the map and the necklace that seemed strangely placed over it.

'Can you see these faint gold lines?' he asked, nudging one of the four gold chains attached to the interlocked pendant. Summer nodded as she saw the finest of gold lines on the map. 'If you line up the chains with the lines then the pendant hangs, not in the centre of the map as you might expect, but here, amongst the west wing secret passageways.'

She leaned over to where he pointed, trying to focus through the scent of cedar from his aftershave, making her lick her lips. He pointed to where the pendant hung. The block handle of the key formed by the two intertwined necklaces created a large rectangular hole through which the chains threaded, allowing the entire key to sit flat against the map. However, the rectangular shape also had a circular cut-out, showing a small and very specific section of the map.

Summer moved the necklace out of the way to see where on the map it had pointed to, but there was nothing there. She tried again, but still she couldn't see anything but the secret passageways that had always been on the map.

She threw up her hands in frustration. 'There's nothing there!'

'With all the hidden journals, the secret maps and the far-flung corners of the world that your sisters have had to travel to, I hardly believe there would be a giant "X marks the spot".'

He was so calmly rational about the whole thing she wanted to scream.

'You've read Catherine's journals a million times. She must have said something in them about the final part of the treasure hunt.'

'It's not a treasure hunt.'

'It kind of is.'

She huffed herself into a chair, wondering why she was fighting this so hard.

'Summer?' Theron asked, coming to crouch in front of her. 'After all the searching and all the stress of the last two months, it's completely understandable to fear that it might all come to nothing.'

Summer angrily wiped at the tear that told them both he was right. She clenched her jaw against the threat of any more tears. 'I'm not this person, Theron. I am rational, deductive, sure.'

'And why is it not okay to be the opposite of those things?' he asked gently. 'Why can't you be all those things *and*…this?'

'Because I'm not the emotional one. That's Star. And Skye's the one in control. So…'

'So, then you are the best of both,' Theron announced as if it were as simple as that. She looked at him and wondered how he could see her as the best of anything. She'd been nothing but trouble since she'd entered his life and couldn't see how she'd be anything less for the rest of it. 'In the meantime, I can't believe that your great-great-great-grandmother would be so meticulous as to plan all this for it to completely fall apart at the end.'

'You can't?'

'No, I have faith.'

Summer huffed out a slightly teary laugh. 'Faith… *Faith!*' she yelled, springing up from the chair and grabbing the journal with the last entry in it.

'Where is it, where is it…yes! Here. Listen. *Faith that all will be well and, most importantly, faith that you will find not just what I have left for you, but what you truly need. For the thing about faith is that while it cannot be seen, it can be felt.* You're right. Faith in what cannot be seen!'

Summer placed the necklace back over the map as Theron had done and carefully made a pen mark in the space in the necklace's ball. She gently swept the necklace out of the way and laughed, rolling her eyes at herself. 'Of course,' she groaned. 'Look,' she said, beckoning Theron to the map.

'What? I don't… Wait, is that—?'

'Catherine's room. It's in the secret passageway just behind Catherine's room.'

She stared up at him, not realising how close they'd become and for the first time not caring. Her heart was soaring with excitement, her pulse racing, and she swept her arms around him and clung on for dear life. Hope, relief, shock and excitement all warred within her and Summer rode out the storm in his embrace.

Theron was sure he could be forgiven for expecting a sliding bookcase or a vase on a table that swung open, rather than the hole in the wall, with fine wooden slats and bits of plaster crumbling onto the floor.

He wanted Summer wearing a face mask. *He* wanted a face mask. There would be at least a century's worth of dust in these passageways, surely. He followed the shadowy outline of Summer created by the beam of her torch as she made her way along the narrow corridor constructed within the walls of the house. The design was ingenious and the construction infallible. He wondered at Catherine, who had made all this happen, and was beginning to think it wise not to underestimate the Soames women.

Summer was trailing her hand against the wall when she came to a stop, and Theron had to pull up quickly to prevent himself from crashing into her. She ran her hand back and forth along the wall on the opposite side of the corridor, frowning, until her eyes widened in shock.

'What is it?' he whispered, not quite sure *why* he was whispering.

'Here, feel this.' She grabbed his hand and he ignored the burn he felt from her touch. It was a heat that his body welcomed, and his heart struggled with.

Spreading his fingers beneath hers, she gently pressed them against the wall and he felt it.

The metal rectangle with a small impression where a key might go. Even he felt a childlike glee at the thought that they might have found the hidden treasure.

'You've found it!' he exclaimed.

She bit her lip, but failed to disguise the smile of pure joy spreading across her features. '*We* found it.' She produced the key and placed it into the lock. The metal slid into place as if it had been used only yesterday. He inhaled in expectation and then…

Nothing. Summer didn't turn the key.

'Summer?'

She leaned forward, pressing her forehead against the door. 'My sisters should be here for this.' She shook her head against the door. 'I can't… I need to wait for them.'

Theron understood. *Family.* He knew why that couldn't be him for Summer, not in this. Star and Skye had gone on this journey with her. It was as much their right as Summer's.

But it didn't stop the twist of hurt slice his heart.

He reached up to where her hand still held the key in the lock and pulled it gently back, taking the key from her loose fingers and hanging the necklace around her neck.

'It's time for you to call them home then,' he said.

CHAPTER EIGHT

SUMMER WANTED TO bottle what she was feeling. She didn't think she'd ever been so excited. Here in this half place where she knew where the diamonds were but hadn't yet seen them. She was on the brink of infinite possibilities and anything and everything she'd ever wanted could happen. Her mother healthy and well, her sisters back with her, she even felt for just a second that she might want to meet her father. That perhaps somehow, being with Theron, they could smooth over old hurts and together they could create something beautiful for the future. She could pinch herself.

There was something about the way that Theron had said she should call her sisters back *home*. Until that moment, the estate had been in the way. It had concealed the one thing they needed to truly help their mother. It had been broken, dusty, old, damp, full of her grandfather's ugliness and his father's, and his grandfather's—Anthony Soames. The man who had married his unwilling cousin for the estate and some jewels, abused her terribly and been miserable until the day he died. There was so much sadness and anger and neglect in this estate.

But there was also Catherine. And Benoit with his secret passages, and even Sheikh Hātem, who Catherine had met in Duratra, had become as much a part of the fabric of the estate as his family had been integral to finding the diamonds. So this time, as she walked through the corridors, instead of the gloom and darkness, she saw the beams of soft sunlight through hazy windows, she saw the potential that was there, just beneath the surface of dust and chaos.

She shook her head. Renovating and repairing the damage to this estate would cost millions and take years. But, even as she discarded the completely impossible idea, her imagination soared as she picked and discarded various styles or materials that could restore the series of problems in the east wing. Her mind jumped ahead to wonder whether Skye's fiancé might be interested and able to help. Then she laughed, wondering what incredible fantastical decoration Star would delve into, what inspiration she would return from the desert with... And in a heartbeat an impression of the estate, restored beyond its former glory to something that honoured both Catherine's history and the Soames sisters' futures, formed in her mind like a miraculous mirage and a longing so deep, so hard took root.

She paused, peering down one of the hallways, and could have sworn she heard the faint echo of children's laughter. She placed a hand over her bump and just for a moment let herself imagine what it might be like to raise her child here. With Theron.

And she could. She could see it so clearly, feel it so powerfully, it made her heart hurt. And it scared her because she'd never wanted anything more in her life.

She found Theron sitting at a table in the garden, leaning back in a chair, his face turned up towards the sun, his features relaxed, and he looked, for the first time, his twenty-eight years. He inclined his head just a little towards her and she realised that was his way of telling her he knew she was there.

She took the seat beside him. 'Do you miss it?' she couldn't help but ask. 'The sun. Greece,' she clarified.

'God, yes. I don't know how you do it. It's…*unhealthy*.'

The laugh tumbled out of her. She was not in the least offended by his over-exaggerated negativity towards England, or Norfolk. It was playful, the teasing. Not mean or cruel. And the idea of him not being able to withstand a bit of English weather was exactly that: laughable. Because there was something incredibly strong, immovable about him. She had—back in Greece—compared him to dolerite and now she realised how fitting that was.

Its powerfully strong properties were what made it so suitable in protective barriers and construction. That was what she felt about Theron. That, no matter what, he would protect her. Perhaps whether she wanted that protection or not.

'So how does it feel?' he asked, cutting through her

thoughts. 'To have found a treasure that's been hidden for over one hundred and fifty years?'

Summer smiled, her heart soaring once again. 'Incredible. But knowing that we'll be able to sell the estate and pay for our mother's treatment is...' She shook her head, trying to find the words that could express the relief, the joy, the hope... 'I know it's not a guarantee that the treatment will work, or that she'll be okay, but it feels as if we've won half the battle at least,' she said truthfully. Although she couldn't quite explain why the thought of selling the estate dimmed her joy a little.

'Catherine Soames must have been a very impressive woman,' Theron mused. 'I can't imagine the thought, determination, the...'

'Faith?' Summer asked as she smiled at him.

'Faith,' he acknowledged with a nod, 'to plan something like this. It must have taken years.'

'I don't know what I'm going to be doing in five years, let alone...' Summer's careless words trailed off and her smile fell as she realised that she would have a four-year-old child. That *they* would have a four-year-old child. She swallowed. She knew they needed to talk about this, but until now she'd been so focused on the diamonds, her mother, even Kyros... Had she thrown them all up as excuses to stop this very conversation? 'I didn't plan for this,' she said, trying to explain.

'I know,' Theron said, looking intently at his hands.

'No, I mean... I had *plans*. Always. Skye was the one who looked after us, Star was the dreamer, the romantic, and I was the one who was going to get *the job*. The one who would make sure we were all going to be okay. Financially.' Summer squinted and it had nothing to do with the gentle sun's rays and everything to do with trying to pierce the shrouds of time to a point when she'd *not* had plans. 'My *plan* was to go to university. Take my fourth year abroad. Finish my degree and find a job in the environmental engineering sector. Get settled. Save money. Look after Mum and the girls.' Summer took a breath, wondering how many years she'd clung to that plan. Nearly ten, maybe? 'And then everything started to fall apart when I found out about Kyros. I deviated from my plan and went to Greece and…' she broke off, laughing bitterly '…and he wasn't there. And then, when he was…' Her heart hurt so much at the memory of his dismissal. She'd never felt such rejection. Until Theron had said what he'd then said. She tried to close the door on that hurt.

She now understood why he'd behaved the way he had. Theron had thought she was a threat to Kyros—the man who had been more of a father to him than he'd had the chance to be to her. And she also had to face the fact that she could have stayed. She *could* have. Theron hadn't the power to kick her out of Greece. Her plan had gone wrong and she'd left because it had been easier than staying and confronting her father.

'The point is,' she pressed on, 'I was making plans. And now I'm not. Because they don't work and I'm not sure what to do any more.' She slowly exhaled the

breath that had built in her chest and wondered if anything she'd said had made sense.

Theron held her gaze when she looked at him. It
was open, accepting and understanding. And suddenly
she didn't want it. She didn't want his understanding.
She wanted him to tell her what to do.

'Plans are not *wants*. Plans are what we do to get
what we want. So, until you know what you want,
you can't make a plan. What do you want?' he asked.

'I want you to tell me what you want,' she hedged.

Theron smiled ruefully and narrowed his eyes as if
considering what to say. 'I want you and our child to
be safe and happy.' But he said it in a way that sounded
sad. As if he was separate from it. And in that moment
Summer didn't have the courage to challenge him on it.

So, what did she want?

The answer was there, beating in her heart. She
wanted the strong, patient, protective man who had not
laughed at her mother's esoteric leanings, who had not
dismissed her job or her interest, who was stubborn
and sometimes sulked like a teenager, but who felt so
deeply he didn't always have the words to describe it.

But something was holding him back. And until
he was able to face that, Summer felt a little too vulnerable to voice the truth in her heart. So instead she
thought of what she wanted for their child and the answer flew from her lips.

'I want you to be there. I want you to be all the
things that my father wasn't or couldn't be. I don't
want our child to hurt the way that I hurt, to feel the
inability or yearning that I felt. I want them to know

who their parents are and be absolutely sure that they are safe. That they are loved. So,' she said, taking a breath, 'I need you to promise that you'll be there.'

When she looked back up at Theron she noticed that his hands were fisted and his knuckles were white, his mouth was a fine tight line, and her heart broke a little. She felt foolish for speaking so freely, but knew that her words had been right and true and she would stand by them for her child.

He nodded once. But to let her know that he'd heard her or in agreement, she couldn't tell. And then he was gone. Just like that. As if he'd never really been sitting there.

Theron paced the length of his room, passing the empty fireplace and unseeing of the dust and damp that had horrified him on his first night here. He felt as if creatures were crawling up his body, scratching against his skin, and he couldn't stop it.

I want you to be there.

She'd had no idea what she'd said, how her words had poked and prodded at the open wound in his heart. He clenched his jaw at the sudden rush of memories, all piling in on each other. Lykos walking away from him, the loss of Althaia, Kyros leaving him behind as he left for the island without him. As if he'd never been a part of the Agyros family. His hand fisted and he wanted to lash out. To punch something. To have a physical pain that would be easier to bear than the chaotically sprawling emotions he couldn't seem to control.

I want you to be all the things that my father wasn't or couldn't be.

He looked at his phone, staring at the five missed calls from Kyros. Theron dropped down onto the mattress and put his head into his hands. Summer still held so much hurt from not knowing Kyros. And what of Kyros? He couldn't imagine what pain it would cause him to have been kept away from his child for so long. He couldn't put it off any more. He had to call Kyros, no matter what it cost him.

Even as he picked up his mobile, Theron couldn't shake the feeling that everything was about to go horribly wrong, just when he needed it to be right.

An hour later Theron stalked through the halls of the estate, knowing that he had to find Summer but feeling utterly out of control. He wanted a tether. He needed her. She had anchored him since the first time he'd seen her. Pulled at his unconscious like a magnet. From the first time he'd got up to leave and sat back down, he'd felt as if he was constantly returning to her, would always return to her, somehow.

She wasn't in the kitchen, or the library. The garden looked empty and he hoped that she wasn't in the secret passageways again. He was about to go back to the upper floors when he thought he heard something being dragged across the floor. It was faint, but there. He followed the strange sound. Whatever it was seemed heavy, which worried Theron. Summer had a habit of biting off more than she could chew.

He turned down a corridor he'd not visited before,

running parallel to the back of the house, seemingly all the way to the other side. The sound finally began to grow louder and the end of the corridor began to throb with light, firing his curiosity. Treading softly, he made his way towards the light, peering around the corner, hoping to remain hidden, but what he saw made his jaw drop.

A floor of aged white and blue tiles stretched down the centre of a large glass-roofed structure attached to the main house. At the far end two thin-paned glass doors were thrown open to the setting sun and in between were huge, deep forest-green plants of all shapes and sizes. Thick, broad leaves bent open like palms, thin, spindly, pale green tendrils coiled and curled, and some kind of climber hung beneath the peeling white ironwork of the ceiling, through which the sun shone beams of dappled light back onto the ornate floor.

'What is this place?' he wondered out loud as he passed into the glass chamber.

'It's the orangery. As the only place utterly ignored by our grandfather, it has—unsurprisingly—thrived,' Summer replied from behind him.

He turned to find Summer hauling an impossibly large sack of compost across the floor. 'What on earth are you doing?'

She peered up at him, huffing a long blonde tendril from her eyes. 'Making a roast dinner. What does it look like I'm doing?'

She was angry. She had every right to be, he knew that, but he felt it too. Anger, frustration. The sense that everything he wanted was right there within his grasp…but not quite.

'You shouldn't be trying to move that,' he declared over his chain of thoughts.

'I *moved* it. I wasn't *trying.*'

Theron suppressed a growl. 'You don't have to do it all yourself, you know.'

'You don't get to do that,' she said, dropping her hold on the enormous plastic bag of compost and rounding on him. 'You don't get to come here, out of nowhere, and suddenly be everything.'

'Be everything?' he asked, the anger in Summer's tone igniting his own.

'I meant be every*where*,' she lied badly. She stepped towards him. 'You might find this hard to believe, but I was fine without you.'

'Yeah?' Theron demanded, taking a step towards her, closing the distance between them like pieces on a chessboard. 'Well, so was I,' he gritted through his teeth, the lie like iron on his tongue, with the realisation that he'd not been even remotely fine until meeting her, even as his mind scrabbled to take the thought back. And that vulnerability, that weakness only angered him more.

His eyes caught hers, the golden sparks firing against the green evidence of her own internal war. And then, as if static electricity arced between them, linking them, drawing them together, he couldn't fight it any more.

They moved together at the same time, lips crashing, hands reaching and curling, hearts beating, breath hitching, caught and held. All of it, he wanted to hold all of it—Summer, their child, the past and the future, in one single breath. To consume it and keep it safe for ever.

She moved against him, her hands reaching around his neck, holding him to her as if worried he would stop. She was like fire, twisting and turning in his arms, and he Prometheus, as if he'd stolen her from the gods themselves and he couldn't help but fear what his punishment would be.

But when she opened her mouth to his, when her tongue thrust against his, all thoughts were lost to sensation. Her fingers moved from curling in his hair to his chest, one hand pulling and the other pressing as if she couldn't tell what she wanted more.

Theron had no such confusion. He wanted everything. The thought roared through his veins, beating like a drum in his chest. He placed his hand at her back, fitting it between her shoulder blades, loving how he could stretch his palm between them, pressing her against him, feeling her chest and thighs against his.

His other hand slipped beneath her shirt and the moment his skin touched hers his heart missed a beat. He thought he felt her gasp against his mouth as his fingers swept around her waist to her stomach, and when his palm pressed against the gentle slope of her abdomen he paused. Gently, she pulled back and gazed up at him—a moment of calm in the madness. A moment just for them that healed a hurt he wasn't sure he'd known was there. But, as they gazed at each other, peace turned to hunger, turned to need, and desire became impossible to resist.

Summer inhaled once swiftly, her eyes inflamed, and she drew him back into her kiss.

She tugged at his jumper, dragging it from him as he tore at the buttons of her shirt. Her hands went to the button on his trousers and his went to her thighs and he lifted her up into his arms. He swallowed the squeak of surprise with his kiss and drew her up his chest, the friction sending enough sparks to consume them both. She shifted endlessly in his arms, and he could have held her there for eternity, but he wanted to touch, to taste, to tease. He backed towards the chaise longue he'd seen—the ancient piece of furniture fitting the faded dignity of the room and completely at odds with what he wanted to do to Summer. He wanted her indecent, he wanted her incandescent, he needed her as mindless with pleasure as he was every time he touched her.

He wanted to hear her scream his name and know that no other man would be able to do that for her. He wanted… The backs of his legs met the cushion of the lounger and he sat, bringing her with him, the air knocked out of their lungs at the impact.

He groaned out loud, not from the fall but from the exquisite pleasure of having her in his arms again. He felt completely lost to her, his heartbeat racing, an urgency in him that he couldn't quite account for. As if time was running out for them and he greedily wanted everything he could take, every memory he could make. It was as if Summer could feel it too. He could sense it in the way she searched his gaze, the way she held onto him so tightly, the desperation that seemed to make their hearts beat together.

Summer had never felt anything like this. As if all the want and need she'd tried to deny had boiled up and escaped and was now coursing through her veins. She was drunk on lust and she felt out of control, as if she honestly didn't know what she would do next. She wasn't this person, she was considered, rational, calm, but right now she was mindless, incoherent and wild. Here in this beautiful orangery, with deep green plants curling up to the ceiling, she felt elemental.

The thought struck her and stuck.

Elemental.

It was as if the word unlocked something within her that freed her from any further doubt, debate, any last vestige that would stop her from doing and taking what she wanted. It was just like it had been that first time in Greece. There was some strange alchemy between her and Theron that seemed to alter her DNA. And that change, that new element that rose within her filled her so completely it took over with the power of a crashing wave.

She pulled back from his hold and slipped her arms from the now damaged shirt, from where he had pulled it apart and sent the buttons flying. Her eyes were on his as his gaze scoured every inch of her skin, flicking back to her every other second as if making sure she was still there. That it wasn't all a dream. She knew how he felt.

She reached for the clasp of her bra and released it, her heart soaring at Theron's swift inhalation and the slash of crimson on his cheeks at the sight of her. She felt glorious. She felt beautiful and womanly and empowered all at the same time. Backing up off the chaise longue, she undid the buttons of her jeans and pushed them from her hips, kicking them out to the side with her bare feet.

He bit his lip and clenched his fists as if he was trying to restrain himself from reaching for her and she loved that she wasn't alone in the madness. Her thumbs hooked in the waistband of her high leg briefs and the gold in his eyes flared. In a second he was half off the sofa, his hands pressing against hers stopping her as she was about to draw them down her thighs.

He looked up at her from a half crouch and her breath caught in her lungs. She felt worshipped. He batted her hands gently aside and slowly, inch by inch, drew the cotton down her thighs. The intimacy of it was overwhelming. As her legs began to tremble she placed a supporting hand against her hip, his fingers sweeping around, and once again she felt cared for and desired at the same time—a combination she'd never experienced before.

She stepped out of her briefs and Theron tucked them into his pocket as if they were something too precious to kick to one side. There she was, naked and vulnerable, while he was dressed only in his dark trousers, the button at the waist she'd undone what felt like hours before.

He gazed up at her as if he were more than happy

to stay there at her feet for as long as she could ever wish it, but that stirring of need, that impatient desire unwound thick and fast in her chest and she reached to pull him up.

When he reached his full height she had to crane her neck to look up at him to take him in, to understand what arcane language their bodies were using to communicate. She wanted to spend the rest of her life learning it, using it and exploring it. She barely had time to register that thought when he swept her up in his arms and took her back to the chaise longue, laying her gently down on it.

He looked at her as if he couldn't get enough. His gaze covered every inch of her and she smiled at the errant thought that he might even turn her over and inspect her back too. The thought brought a blush to her cheeks, one that his keen gaze didn't miss. He opened his mouth as if he was about to ask her, but then shook his head as if he forgot what he'd intended, lost in the sight of her, his eyes glazed with the same desire and lust that she felt coursing through her body. Rather than the frantic desperation of moments before, the thick heavy thump of need pulsing in her veins became slow and languorous, as if they had both been hypnotised by the same thing.

He leaned back on his heels and reached for her foot, picking it up gently and bending to place kisses along the arch. Unconsciously, she pulled her leg back slightly, the sensation driving a laugh from her lungs and drawing him towards her and exposing her in a way that caught her breath. His hands swept up her thigh, his kisses following, open-mouthed and deliciously decadent as her heart thundered in her chest and he gently pressed her thigh to the side.

Her back arched off the mattress the moment his tongue pressed against her, and her hand fisted over her mouth to prevent herself from crying out. She had barely caught her breath when another long sweep of his tongue drove the oxygen from her lungs and her back into the air once again. She cursed, unable to stop herself, and she swore she could tell that he was smiling.

He pressed gently against her pelvis, angling himself and her into a position that allowed him to—

Her mind completely blanked. She couldn't have said what he did, she didn't know, other than it was amazing and incomprehensible and in the space of a heartbeat she was completely overcome by an orgasm that she felt broken by.

She came back round to the feel of gentle kisses around her abdomen, something about them bringing a sweet tear to her eye that she dashed away before Theron could see.

Eventually, as if reluctantly, the kisses began to move up her body, along her ribcage, Theron's head gently nudging at her side, causing her to shift onto her side so that he could slip behind her and place more kisses on her shoulder blades as his hands wound around her protectively.

The hot humidity of the orangery was the absolutely perfect temperature to be there naked in his arms. Her heart felt light, happy but scared, as if this moment was precious only because it might not last.

She felt his forehead lean against her shoulder.

'I don't have a condom,' he said, his tone regretful but not more than that.

She sighed, unable to help the smile curving her lips. 'I think it's a bit late for that, Theron.'

There was a pause before he replied. 'There is no risk from me. I have not been with anyone since you.'

She swallowed, realising the thought of risk hadn't crossed her mind. Even in this, she marvelled, he was protecting her. 'Me too. I...' Her words trailed off as his fingers entwined with hers, reassuring, loving even. She turned back to look at him, his gaze burning bright and intense. And, just like that, want and desire ignited in a firestorm and she reached for him, knowing he was the only thing that would quench her need.

They made love until the stars disappeared from the night sky and the sun peered at them from over the horizon. A gentle yellow glow filled the glass-walled room, warming the jasmine until its perfumed scent filled the air. Summer pulled the large throw Theron had found at some point during the night over her shoulders and burrowed deeper into his embrace. She thought he was asleep, but a new tension filled his form, an energy that ignited her own and for a moment she indulged in it. A moment where heady desire, expectation and promise were just there in the next heartbeat, if she could only—

In the distance she could hear the ring of Theron's

mobile and they stilled, holding their breath, as if instinctively they both knew.

Knew that something was about to happen that would change everything.

CHAPTER NINE

THERON WAS WAITING in her room for her when she came out of the shower. Her steps faltered when she saw his broad shoulders outlined by the early morning sun. He appeared to be looking out of the window, but she was half convinced it was to protect her modesty.

'You should wear the green dress,' he stated without looking at her.

And in an instant the fury that she'd banked with cool water from the shower reignited. 'Calling Kyros was bad enough. You don't get to tell me what to wear too,' she threw at him.

Theron's shadowy outline bowed his head. 'He needed to know.'

'Will you always put his needs before mine? Before yours?'

Frustration bloomed over anger like a watercolour painting. They had just been getting somewhere. There were things they still needed to say. But now Kyros was twenty minutes away her thoughts had completely scattered.

'You sound like Lykos.' Theron's tone was dark, but not bitter or resentful.

Summer felt seasick. She just wasn't sure what she should be feeling, where her allegiance should be. With Mariam? Her father? Or the father of her child? The man she knew she was falling in love with. Nerves tickled her soul.

What if Kyros didn't like her? What if he became angry with her mother? What if she didn't like him? Theron clearly respected him, loved him even—he'd cared for his wife throughout her illness and part adopted two teenage tearaways. So he couldn't be *bad*.

But she couldn't shake the feeling that meeting her father would cost Theron something. Cost *them* something. No matter what happened, it would definitely alter his relationship with the man who had been like a father to him for longer than his own parents were alive. And Theron had still made the call to Kyros.

For her, she realised. It was a sacrifice he'd made. For her.

'Theron—'

The sound of a car on the gravel drive turned both their heads towards the window.

'He's here,' Theron announced needlessly, and he looked back at her before leaving. 'The green dress. You will look beautiful in it.'

Theron made it to the doorway as the sleek racing-green Jeep pulled to a stop in front of the stone steps. He felt numb. As if he'd gone into shock ahead of some great trauma, as if protecting himself from what would come.

Kyros stepped out of the vehicle and straightened his tie. Despite the fact that his hair and beard were shocking white, they were thick and vital. No one ever mistook Kyros for a weak old man. At full height they stood shoulder to shoulder and, despite the immense power he wielded, Kyros had always been quick to laugh and his heart was huge.

But it was a heart that, once wounded, rarely recovered and when Kyros looked Theron straight in the eye, Theron knew. Any hope he might have entertained that they could survive this, that their relationship would survive, was gone.

Kyros looked at the house and for a fleeting moment he seemed scared, before he returned his steely gaze to Theron.

Theron opened his mouth to speak but was cut off.

'We will speak later. My daughter?' Kyros demanded, wanting to know she was here.

Theron nodded, but before he took Kyros inside he needed to know. Theron forced the words out through clenched teeth. 'She is pregnant.'

Kyros's steely gaze turned glacial. 'Yours?'

'Naí.'

With nothing left to say, Theron led Kyros into the house. Summer had said that she'd be in the library and each step towards her felt inexplicably as if it were taking him away from her. He had to put a hand out to steady himself, vertigo hitting him as if he'd entered an Escher painting.

* * *

Summer had hastily slipped into the green dress and pinned her hair up, let it down and put it back up again in the time since Theron had left her room. She was in the library now, finally deciding on hair up because she was so hot and flustered she needed it off her neck. To stop herself from pacing she'd sat in the chair, but the moment she heard footsteps in the corridor she lurched up, her hands clasped before her.

Suddenly she wanted to cry. But she fisted her hands, ordering herself to be strong. She was aware that two men stood in the doorway, yet she only had eyes for one. Kyros—her father—looked so familiar she had to sit down. Kyros covered the room in strides as if worried that she was unwell, his arm at her side, ready to support her, which she gratefully took.

'I'm sorry,' she said, embarrassed by her reaction.

'There is *nothing* that you could be sorry for.' His reply was strong and sincere, his eyes wide as if he just couldn't look at her long enough. She knew the feeling because it was exactly how she felt. He pulled up a seat so he could hold her hand. '*I* am the one who is sorry and I cannot even begin to ask for your forgiveness. I only hope that you believe I truly did not know of your existence.'

Summer smiled through a watery gaze that hungrily consumed every single inch of the man who had fathered her, yet not been her father. 'I know. Mum always said that you didn't know.' She pressed her lips together at the mention of her mother. She didn't miss the way that Kyros's blue gaze sparked, but not with anger, something more like surprise before it was quickly mastered.

'We have so much to talk about,' Kyros insisted, pulling his chair closer to hers.

'We have time,' Summer said, a slight pinprick of hurt cutting deep at her heart, wondering whether the same could be said for her mother. She couldn't stop staring at him. Her eyes raked over him, wondering that he was really there. Wondering at this strange sense of connection she felt branded into her heart in an instant.

'Your mother, Mariam. How is she?' Kyros asked in a way that made Summer think he already knew. Summer turned to the doorway, wanting to see if Theron had said anything, but he wasn't there.

She frowned, but returned her attention to Kyros and took a deep breath. 'She is not well.' Her father seemed to clench his jaw, as if bracing himself. 'But we are soon going to be able to get her the treatment she needs.'

'We?'

'Yes,' Summer said, her smile wide and full of love. 'Me and my sisters.'

Kyros nodded. 'You have sisters. That is good. You have…' he seemed to search for the words '…you have had a good life?' he asked tentatively.

'Yes. So very good,' she said sincerely and reassuringly. 'I never blamed you. Mum made it very clear that you would have moved heaven and earth if you'd known about me. But…' Summer hesitated, not wanting to paint her mother in a bad light '…she…she told me that she didn't know your full name and how to find you.'

Confusion passed into realisation in her father's gaze and a nod that reminded her of Theron seemed to conclude his thoughts.

'I would like to tell you how we met,' he began. 'I don't want to...contradict or say anything your mother wouldn't want you to know, but... I want to be honest,' he said, shrugging into the words as if feeling his own way through this strange situation.

Summer nodded and as they huddled together he explained how he had met Mariam Soames.

'I was on one of the islands. I had gone there by myself in order to figure some things out. My wife, Althaia—I loved her greatly. We had been together since we were sixteen and twice that many years later our love was still strong. It was a soft, gentle kind of love, but one that was unbreakable.' His eyes misted for a moment and Summer put her hand on his. 'We had just found out her diagnosis and our world had been shattered. Althaia had asked me to leave to give us both some time to process how we felt.

'I was...devastated. Selfish. Hurt. Angry,' Kyros admitted, shaking his head at himself. 'Your mother, Mariam. She...burst into my life at that moment and, somehow, took it all away. Before I even knew her name, I—' He clenched his jaw, seemingly to stop himself from saying more. 'I told your mother. Everything. About Althaia and her diagnosis, our marriage. She told me about the loss of the partner that she was still grieving, about her daughters and the love she felt for them. She was so…bright and fierce. She was like a whirlwind and I couldn't help but be drawn in. Somehow, together, we found more than solace in each other, and I need you to know that what we shared…it was incredibly special to me.' Summer looked at him as his gaze clouded with memories and unspoken moments, before it cleared enough for him to carry on. 'We agreed, nothing more than that one week together, but it's important that you know it changed my life.

'The moment I returned home I told my wife about Mariam. Althaia's understanding was as surprising to me as my short time with Mariam. Althaia understood the kind of love we shared was different and that the future we would have was not for a moment what anyone could ever imagine or choose. But I did. Each and every day, I chose that life and her love and I would do it again in a heartbeat. But it was your mother who helped me make that choice.'

He gazed at her with watery eyes, the sincerity and truth shining in them warming her through.

'Mari and I—'

'Mari?'

He smiled, as if embarrassed by the name he had given her mother. '*Mariam*—' he stressed for her benefit '—and I knew that what we shared, even for that brief moment, was special but could not be. I had Althaia, she had her daughters… We felt as if it had been a gift of sorts. One that we could carry within us for ever, but not something to be revisited.

'I thought at one point…' He trailed off and Summer searched his face for a conclusion, until Kyros shook his head and any possible ending away. He sighed deeply. 'But I am here now. And so are you!' The exclamation lifted his features from darker memories and she thought she recognised some of herself in him once again. She lifted her hand to sweep aside a tendril of blonde hair that had fallen from the band and Kyros's eyes caught on her collarbone. 'Oh.'

She immediately pressed her hand over it, protectively rather than secretively.

'You have the family birthmark?' He laughed, surprised and pleased.

'Yes. It was how I first realised you were my...' The word, so strange and unused, sat on her tongue.

'Father. Yes, Summer. I am your father.'

She had waited her entire life for those words, half convinced she'd never hear them, never feel this bond that welled up between them, surrounding them, binding them together, and tears brimmed in her eyes.

'You were in Thiakos's apartment. Five months ago?'

'Yes.'

'I...' His head hung down. 'I am ashamed. I did not know who you were. An urgent business deal had brought me back from the island and I—'

'Please. You don't have to explain. What happened with Theron—'

'No. Let's not discuss that now. I will deal with him later.' Summer frowned, worried, but not wanting to contradict or push things with Kyros when things were so fresh and new. He took her hands in his and held them tight. 'There is so much I want to tell you. So much history you have back home in Greece. Perhaps, when things are settled, you could come and visit.'

'I'd like that very much,' she replied, feeling a wetness against her cheek that he reached up to brush away. His hand paused and he looked to her, seeking permission, and when she nodded his thumb swept away the tear and she leaned into his palm as if it had always been there.

Theron looked out across the impossibly flat Norfolk horizon that seemed incredible to him. It gave the sky so much space that it seemed further away than ever, so untouchable that it made his chest hurt.

He was unused to the silence and it was unnerving. It gave rise to too many thoughts—thoughts that were on the future now. Summer had her father. When she and her sisters found the Soames diamonds and sold the estate, Summer would be more than financially secure. She had their love and support. She would be protected by them, her family. And Kyros would make sure that she never wanted for a single thing.

But not him.

Because he couldn't give her the one thing she wanted. It ate at his soul, scratched and lashed out like a living thing, breathing fire and burning everything it touched.

I want you to be there.

Bitter breath fell from his lips. He hadn't even been there for Kyros. He'd lied to the old man, kept him from his daughter. He had taken her virginity and kicked her out of his life as if she were less than nothing. And now she was pregnant.

Theron fisted his hands, impatient for Kyros to return, because he knew what was coming. He'd seen it when the old man had looked at him as if he were a stranger. Family meant everything to Kyros. And he was not part of Kyros's family.

She is your family.

He rejected the thought that sounded far too much like Althaia, making his heart hurt all the more. He felt torn between the absolute desire, a need so powerful it rocked his foundations, to be there for Summer. With her and their child. But he couldn't. He couldn't make that promise. Even the thought of it tore his heart, his pulse pounding, a cold sweat tickling his neck.

The breath left his lungs, burning as it did, as he thought of what he would miss. Watching Summer grow big and round with their child. The quick change of her temper, from ridiculous anger to tears, to a laugh so pure it healed everything. The way she'd look at the world as if everything was wondrous and worth study, worth investigation. He'd miss the moment of her success when she was able to find the jewels with her sisters. The moment that her mother would receive the treatment she needed, and the moment Summer realised that it had worked. That it had all been worth it. In his mind's eye, Theron saw her future, full of love and laughter and sunshine. And he wasn't in it.

She had everything she needed now. Her father. Her mother. The diamonds. There was nothing for him to give her other than promises he couldn't keep.

The sound of the Jeep's engine firing drew Theron back to the present and he looked up to find Kyros standing at the top of the stone steps.

'She's incredible,' Kyros said, as if in wonder at his daughter.

'She is,' Theron agreed.

'I looked for her mother once.'

Theron frowned in confusion.

Kyros sighed. 'I...thought you might have known because of Lykos, but this surprises you?'

'I had no idea. I didn't...' He clenched his jaw, hating the words he forced from his lips. 'I didn't believe her. When she first told me.'

Kyros nodded, looking out over the estate's long driveway, squinting in the sun. And, without another word, he got into the Jeep and drove away.

Summer was looking for Theron. Meeting her father had been beyond anything she could have imagined. It had healed a part of her that had ached since first finding the photo and soothed a part of her that had hurt for years.

She had just got off the phone with her mother and felt strangely as if everything was falling into place. Mariam had been shocked, yes, but Summer hadn't missed the hope and the yearning in her mother's voice. As if she still thought of Kyros, still cared for him. Mariam had been desperate to explain that she had kept Kyros's identity secret out of respect for his wife. It had been her decision to embark on that affair and she had hated the thought of Summer or Al-

thaia suffering because of it. And even though she'd
hated lying to Summer she had honoured the promise
she had made to him. Mariam told her that she had
always intended to tell her one day, but somehow that
day had just got further and further away. She'd pep-
pered Summer with questions about Kyros, and was
startled by her response.

'He will be in England for a while and I was hoping that you would come up to Norfolk. We have some
news and I would like you and Kyros to be part of that.'

Her mother had agreed instantly, but Summer had
been distracted because she'd seen Theron through the
window, looking out at her father's car driving away.

As she turned towards the estate's entrance Summer
decided that she didn't want to be like her parents—two
people who clearly had strong feelings for each other
but had missed so much. She was happy that Kyros had
stayed with Althaia, that the love they'd shared had accepted and moved beyond his affair with her mother. But
the thought of that lost time was like a pull on her heart.

She didn't want that with Theron. She didn't want
to miss another minute with him. Because, even when
they were arguing, he seemed to understand her. Even
when he teased her, he taught her something about
herself. And it was more than that…it was *him*. She
wanted to know *him*. She wanted to help soothe the
hurts she felt were just beneath the surface. His inse-
curity about his place with Kyros, the loss of his relationship with a man who was still like a brother to
him even after ten years of silence—and the deepest
pain of the loss of his parents. She wanted to help him

heal. She wanted him to see what she saw in him. She wanted him to see…how much she loved him.

She drew to a stop, her hand covering her mouth in shock. *She loved him.*

The man who yelled at her for trying to drag compost across the floor, the man whose eyes didn't glaze over when she talked about her work, who could see how important her independence was, who understood her need to be responsible and accountable to and for herself. The man who had brought her to dizzying heights of pleasure, the man who was the father of her unborn child. He had asked her to marry him once and she had said no. But now it was all she could think of.

She burst through the front doors of the house, hoping that he would still be standing where she had seen him from the window, but he wasn't. She turned, looking out to the road, her heart thumping with the need to see him, to tell him. Not just about what had happened with her father, but her feelings for him. Her love.

She was teary from happiness and she couldn't wait to share it with Theron. He had brought this to her. He had brought her father to her and given her hope and a sense of more than she could ever imagine.

A little voice in her head told her to slow down, to hold back, to pull back from the edge, when all she wanted to do was hurl herself over it with blind faith and love. Maybe her head had been turned by Catherine's journals, a treasure hunt and what she secretly believed was a reunited love between her parents, but all this…*happiness*…she didn't think she'd felt it before.

Theron was at the table they had sat at yesterday and, when he saw her, his eyes raked over her hotly as if he'd never seen anything more beautiful and she felt so utterly precious. Until he blinked and the look was gone. She frowned, rubbing her arms against the sudden bite to the westerly wind, and her steps slowed as she approached. It was as if a cloud had passed over the sun and she resisted the urge to shiver.

He sat there, unmoving, as if he were cut from a piece of dark marble, eyes watching her in one long gaze, taking her in completely. She halted on the other side of the table, suddenly uncomfortable. She could see his jaw flexing from here.

'Theron—'

'How was it?' he pressed out through teeth she was sure were clenched.

She looked about the garden, trying to find signs for why it felt as if everything was strange all of a sudden. Off-kilter, as if she were in a dark, twisted, kaleidoscope version of her world.

'It was…amazing,' she hedged, not able or willing to lie. 'He…is beyond what I'd hoped. He wants to see Mum,' she admitted, unable to prevent the hope in her voice. 'And I can't thank you enough. For calling him. Bringing him here,' she said, hoping that the sincerity in her voice, the truth of it would penetrate this strange, hard outer shell he seemed to have retreated behind. Her stomach twisted as she realised that something bad must have happened between him and Kyros.

'Theron, did something—'

'It's good. That he wants to see your mother.'

She frowned at his responses, his actions, all just a little delayed. She felt out of step with him in a way that she'd never done before. Giving up all pretence, she rushed round the table and went to him, kneeling on the floor, her hands reaching for his, uncaring of how desperate or needy she might look.

'Theron, in the last week…' She struggled to find the words. His lack of response, the way he looked at her as if he couldn't comprehend her behaviour, was awful in comparison to how she'd always felt understood by him. She huffed out a breath, shook her head a little and said, 'Theron, ask me to marry you again.' The smile pulling at her lips, the sparkle she could feel in her eyes hung on a heartbeat. And as if she could sense him withdrawing even in her silence, she leant upwards, reaching for him, and pressed kisses against firm, unyielding lips.

It was then that she realised her heart was already breaking. It had cracked just a little each minute since she'd seen him sitting at the table. And still she kissed him. Again and again, hoping that he'd open beneath her. Wishing that he'd let her in.

Finally, he reached up to her hands to pull them free from his neck and leaned away from her, that dark hollow look in his eyes. And this time she wasn't able to prevent the shiver that trembled through her body.

'Ask me to marry you,' she whispered. 'Please, just—'

'No, Summer.'

And her heart shattered.

'Why?' she asked, not quite sure she wanted to know the answer.

'I could ask the same question,' he said, his tone devoid of emotion. She stood up and frowned at him, stepping away from him, wondering why the sun she felt against her skin wasn't warming her.

'What?' she asked. 'Why I want you to ask me to marry you?' He nodded. 'Because I…' The words felt silly now. Strange. Even though in her heart she knew it was the truth, saying them to him now when he was being like this felt wrong. 'I want us to be a family,' she replied eventually.

Her stomach dropped as she looked at his face, and she knew somehow that she'd said absolutely the wrong thing. But, before she could take it back, Theron stood from the chair and turned his back on her as if unable to look at her any more. The ground beneath her feet shifted and Summer couldn't work out what had happened. When had everything gone so wrong?

'You have a family, Summer. Your sisters, your mother… Kyros.'

'Is that what this is about? My father?'

Theron took her question and turned it in his mind. Was it about Kyros? It might have started out like that, trying to protect Kyros from Summer and then to protect the old man from Theron's own mistake.

Liar. You were protecting yourself then, just like you are now.

No!

Theron knew how much growing up without Kyros

had hurt Summer, he knew what she wanted, what she needed. Stability, safety, security…she'd asked him to make that promise and he just couldn't. A part of him knew that he was being irrational, but the feral part, the animal instinct was flooding him with the need to flee. It felt visceral and all-consuming and he shook with the effort to fight it.

I want us to be a family.

He'd wanted that for so long. For ever. But he couldn't… Images of his parents' fear-filled eyes, of Althaia's, full of pain, of Lykos's hurt and anger, turning away from him, and his heart turned in on itself.

'No,' he said, having to clear his throat, finding the strength for what he needed to do. 'This has nothing to do with Kyros,' he said, turning to hold her gaze, surprised at the numbness settling over his body. 'You have what you need now, Summer. You have the diamonds, your mother will receive her treatment and you will be supported by your family. Kyros will ensure that none of you will want for anything ever again.'

'But I want *you*,' she said, her words bouncing off the barriers around his heart. 'I *love* you.' A distant part of him recognised the panic, the hurt flooding her expressive features, but that numbness was too strong. 'Can't you see that?'

'You can't see love,' he retorted.

'Neither can you see faith,' she returned instantly.

'So you think you love me? In a matter of days?' he scoffed, wondering at his own cruelty.

'In a matter of *moments*,' she replied determinedly.

As if somehow his dismissal of her had only made her stronger. 'From the moment I saw you I—'

He shook his head, the act cutting her off mid-sentence. He was glad. He didn't want to hear the rest of what she had to say. He knew instinctively that he would bring out those words to torture himself in years to come. When he thought of her. When he thought of their child.

Would his child feel the same sense of loss as Summer had done? As he himself had done? The ground beneath his feet jerked, but he ignored it. No. She and Kyros would make sure that the child wanted for nothing, including love.

As if her thoughts began to follow the same path as his, her hands flew to her stomach as if to protect it from their words. Their hurt.

She looked up at him, her eyes watery but glinting with something else. Something fearfully like understanding.

'I think…' she said, her breath shuddering through her words as if she were fighting to say them. 'I think…' she tried again '…that you are scared.' His scoff gave her pause, but she pressed on. 'I think that you have experienced great loss and hurt over the years and that…that the idea of family is terrifying to you.'

'Summer—' he warned.

'I think that this family is something you want so much that it terrifies you.'

He turned away, unable to look at the truth shining in her eyes as she spoke. From over his shoulder, he heard her words.

'So I don't need a promise from you that you'll be there for me. I'm promising to be here for you.'

He took a step away from her, the anguish in his heart so severe that he feared he'd never recover.

'I will *always* be here for you,' she said as he took a second step and a third. And just as he reached the car he could have sworn that he heard her say, 'I love you.'

'Oh, Summer, when did this happen?' Skye asked.

Summer held back a sob and looked at her hands. 'A couple of hours ago.'

'Oh, hun!' Star cried, pulling her into a hug that Skye quickly added herself to.

Summer let herself sink into her sisters' embrace for a moment, indulging in their comfort. She'd meant what she'd said to him. She did have faith that he would come back to her. That he loved her. But there, in their arms, she allowed herself to accept the possibility that he might not be able to overcome the traumas of his past.

'You're sure he's going to come back?' Skye asked and Summer nodded, blinking away the tears.

'And if he doesn't?' Star tentatively asked.

'Then we will be fine,' Summer insisted, pulling her head up from the hug to speak and lock eyes with her sisters. 'Mum raised us all on her own. And I have you both. And we'll find these damned diamonds and sell the estate to Lykos and Mum can be receiving treatment as quickly as the beginning of next week. And then—*then* I can make a plan.'

'What about uni?' Star asked, her eyes glistening with sympathetic tears.

'I'll take a few years' sabbatical,' Summer replied, her own eyes glistening. Not with regret, but determination. 'This is the twenty-first century, and I can and will have my child, my education *and* my dream job.'

After a beat, her sisters sent up squeals of delight and cheered, Star started to dance and when Skye turned to watch her, laughing, Summer allowed herself just a moment of hurt that Theron wasn't there to witness her family's joy for her. Because now the ache in her heart wasn't just for herself, it was for him. It was for the damage done by his childhood that held him back from being all that he could be, feeling all that he could feel.

As she looked up at her sisters, celebrating her pregnancy, the culmination of their journey to find the Soames diamonds, their heritage, their mother's future health and the love that had inspired it all, Summer felt and saw the richness of life. She understood why Catherine had protected the jewels from a husband who would most likely have sold them. She understood too how Catherine had embraced the love she had felt for Benoit and Hātem, despite the heartache. How she had used it to give her the strength she'd needed in her marriage and her motherhood. Summer looked around the room and felt the Soames heritage rise up, as if generations of Soames women were here to witness and celebrate yet another of their line.

She allowed a tear at the thought of having to sell the estate to roll down her cheek—she would give it that—

knowing that she would take their heritage with them forward into their new future, with their mother's health secured and her sisters' happiness assured.

'Let's do it,' she announced.

Skye frowned. 'Do what?'

'Find the diamonds!'

'What, now?' Star asked. 'It's five-thirty in the morning,' she replied as if Summer had lost her mind.

'We've been talking all night?' Summer asked, shocked.

'Yes!' Star and Skye announced together, laughing.

'I'm so sorry,' Summer said, thinking of how tired they would all be.

'Don't be,' Skye said. 'It's been a while since we stayed up like that. I've missed it.'

'And I've missed you,' Summer said, looking between Skye and Star. 'The last couple of years, it's felt a little like we've all been drifting apart.' She'd been scared to say it, but breathed a sigh of relief as she saw on their faces that her sisters felt the same way. She reached for their hands, a smile of joy pulling at her lips. 'And now you're going to be living in France, and you in Duratra... Everything's changing,' she said, her voice soft with wonder. 'But that's okay. We don't always have to have a plan, we don't always have to see our path. Sometimes, we just need a bit of faith.'

This time Star laughed. 'Who are *you* and what have you done with Summer?' she demanded.

'I am your sister,' she said, the tears welling once again. 'And I'm going to need both of you to help me so much in the next few years.'

'Whatever you need,' said Star.

'Whenever you need it,' said Skye.

Staring into the flames of the fireplace in Lykos's London townhouse, Theron bowed his head, his fists clenched against the pain that still rocked his body from Kyros's dismissal of him from his life. From his own personal exile from Summer's life. But this time, instead of fighting it, he chose to feed the anger instead. The fury coursing through his veins at what had happened after and at what had happened so many years before collided, and he glared up at Lykos.

'You knew,' Theron growled.

Lykos's silvery gaze narrowed ever so slightly before he nodded firmly, confirming the accusation.

'You knew that Kyros had an illegitimate child— *Summer*—and that is why you left all those years ago?'

Lykos looked away, as if debating how to handle him.

'No, I'm done, Lykos. No more evasions, no more lies or witty rebukes. No more. I want the truth. All of it.'

Lykos turned his steely gaze on Theron, the anger burning like phosphorous in his eyes. 'You want the truth? Fine. When I was nineteen, Kyros asked me to go looking for Mariam Soames. He didn't tell me why, but I wasn't stupid. A Greek billionaire tycoon looking for a young Englishwoman and all he had was a faded photo?' Lykos got up out of his chair and stalked over to the window, the sun beginning to rise across the London skyline. 'He had betrayed Althaia! He had betrayed his family!' Lykos raged.

Theron might have flinched but his own anger was simmering. 'So you discovered Summer's existence, and what—just abandoned them?'

'No. Over the years, I have checked up on them. Made sure they were okay.'

'Really? So, Mariam Soames' stage three cancer diagnosis just slipped through the gaps then?' Theron demanded. 'The way that Summer constantly worries about money, about paying her sisters back for all they have sacrificed for her to attend university?' Theron spat before rising out of his chair to face Lykos. 'A girl who thinks that spending one hundred euros on a dress for herself is an extravagance she doesn't deserve, Lykos. You've drunk more than that this evening alone!'

'I didn't know about the cancer,' Lykos roared back. 'I'm going to buy the estate!'

Theron shook his head in disgust. 'Were you? Why did you call me, Lykos? The truth this time.'

'I recognised her, that night in the restaurant. I knew who she was. But what I didn't recognise was the way you looked at her. Because I've *never* seen you look at a woman like that. And I know—or I *thought* I knew—how you would feel if she were pregnant.'

'What do you mean, *thought* you knew?'

'I believe it's time for you to tell me just what the hell you think you're doing here with me instead of being with *her*,' Lykos spat disdainfully. Theron could see it as Lykos paced back and forth in front of the fireplace—the anger that he had been keeping at bay all evening.

'What is it to you?' Theron demanded, wanting it. Relishing it.

In the blink of an eye, Lykos spun round, grabbed Theron by the shirt collar and shoved him up against the wall. 'You walked away from them!' he roared, the fury in his eyes blazing as strongly as the hot coals in Theron's gut. 'You know where we came from and you *walked away*?'

Theron shoved both palms into Lykos's chest, pushing him back, but not as far as he'd have liked. 'Yes!' he roared back, stepping forward and closing the space he'd just created between them. His blood pounded in his veins, his hands fists already and desperate for a fight, for the sting of physical pain to overshadow the emotional wound that he'd opened up in himself and he feared would never heal.

'How dare you?' Lykos growled.

Theron shoved again and the look on Lykos's face was thunderous. But also knowing.

'What does it matter to you, Lykos?' he demanded.

'Because your parents *died*, Theron. But mine left. They—as you have done—*chose* to leave.' The disgust written on his face was so much worse than his anger. 'And you have *no* idea what that feels like.'

'No? Like when *you* chose to leave?'

'I asked you to come with me. *You* chose *him*.'

'I chose family, Lykos. I chose Althaia and Kyros. And…' Theron clenched his jaw, a wave of grief hitting him hard and threatening to pull him under '…you didn't even come to the funeral.' His eyes felt hot and wet and he had to turn away.

'I was there.' Lykos's words were a low whisper. 'I was there, Theron. I just…didn't come close enough for you to see. How could you think I wouldn't be?'

'Because everyone leaves, Lykos. Everyone. My parents, you, Althaia. And when Summer asked me to promise to be there—to give her the one thing her father had not been able to give her… I just couldn't. I've hurt enough. It's easier to let her go.'

'So she was right. You are scared? Theron—' Lykos started, but Theron interrupted, not wanting to hear what his friend had to say.

'No. I'm done. With the lot of you,' Theron said, turning away and grabbing his suit jacket.

'Then you are not the man I thought you were,' Lykos accused.

Theron paused. Jaw clenched, hands fisted, all that anger and hurt so very close to the surface.

'I called you because I knew she was pregnant. I called you because I knew how much you cared for her and I knew how much you would love both her and your child. But love isn't anything without faith. And I was hoping she'd have taught you that.'

'Faith?'

The words so familiar, bound up in a one-hundred-and-fifty-year-old treasure hunt that had nothing to do with him, struck a chord and held him still.

'Faith that it's worth it. Faith that her love for you is more powerful than the hurt that you *might* feel,' Lykos demanded.

While faith can't be seen, it can be felt.

Theron shook the words from his memory.

'And you love her?'

'Yes, of course,' he admitted, his head bowed.

'Then you are a fool and you don't deserve her at all.'

Theron rounded on Lykos, fury spreading through his chest.

'No,' Lykos pressed. 'You don't get to have it both ways. You can't love her and turn your back on her and your child because you're scared, Theron. Be better than my parents. Be better than me, dammit, and I swear…if I have to say one more soppy thing to get you to realise that you need to go back and fight for her, I'll kill you myself,' he finished, angrily throwing his hands into the air and turning to pour himself another drink.

Theron couldn't help the laugh that launched from his chest, cutting through the tension and the anger. It cracked something within him, letting something free. Something powerful, strong, bright and healing.

'I'm not joking, Theron. If you tell anyone what I've just said, I'll hunt you down,' Lykos threatened, pointing at him with his whisky glass. 'Sit down,' he ordered.

'Why?'

'Because you need a plan.'

'A plan?'

'Do I have to do everything for you, brother? To win her back, of course.'

* * *

The sisters crept through the tunnel, Summer in the lead, jumping at every little sound, and laughing at themselves.

'Why is this so creepy?' Star asked in a whisper.

'Why are you whispering?' Skye asked, also in a whisper.

Summer felt the childlike giggle rumble in her chest. She felt drunk. Drunk on love and excitement— all the more sweet for the underlying ache that felt as if it would always be there until Theron came back to her.

If.

No. She wouldn't think like that.

She held the key in one hand and the torch in the other and came to a stop, her sisters stumbling a little.

'Aren't we on the other side of Catherine's bed-room?'

'Yup,' Summer confirmed with a smile.

'All this time!'

Skye shushed Star as Summer found the lock and retrieved the key. The last time she'd been here was with Theron. He had been so close she had felt—

'Summer?'

'Sorry.' Summer shook the memories from her head and pushed the key and turned, this time gently pressing against a door that swung inward as easily as if it had been used only yesterday. She cast a glance to her sisters and, holding out her hand for Skye, who held out her hand for Star, they made their way through the door.

The torch illuminated a room large enough for them

all to stand, albeit slightly hunched. There were shelves on the walls lined with books that Star was instantly drawn to, and Skye's torch beam passed thoroughly over every inch of the room as if properly inventorying the space. But Summer was drawn to a table beneath a once-white dustsheet and when she gingerly lifted the sheet she saw three velvet-covered boxes on it.

'Summer?'

She removed the sheet and her sisters huddled around as Summer lifted the first box, the smallest of the three. At her sisters' encouraging nods she raised the lid and in the torch's beam three diamonds sparkled so much that she had to blink. Perched between the folds was the most beautiful ring she'd ever seen, pristinely preserved and absolutely breathtaking. All the sisters lost their breath simultaneously. Gingerly, Skye reached for the second box and Star the third, as Summer placed the torch on the floor facing up to illuminate the small space better. Star's box was deeper and narrow, and when she lifted the lid she gasped at the sight of the large diamond in the centre of an exquisitely detailed diadem. And when Skye opened the box she held to reveal a stunning necklace the rush of air from her lungs drew the gazes of her sisters and they each sighed, as if stunned by the sheer opulence and beauty that Catherine had hidden away.

A longing rose in Summer's chest, a want that rivalled the way she felt about Theron, but different. Sadder. She would love to have kept these pieces. Not because of their financial value but their emotional one. It was as if each of the sisters was taking a moment, remembering the journeys that had brought them here. All they'd wanted was to fund their mother's treatment, and now they would be able to do that.

But Summer had sensed a change in her siblings. Their journeys had done more than bring them here. They had changed, and not because of the men they'd met and now loved, but because of the women they had become. Women who were worthy of this inheritance, as Catherine had known they would be. And it was there, in a secret room created by their great-great-great-grandmother, she felt as if something had been righted in the world, felt the sigh of relief that came when something had found its true home.

She allowed that feeling to fill her, even as she knew that within hours, after meeting Mr Beamish, the estate lawyer, she would be arranging for the sale of the estate, and it hurt. A layer added over the ache caused by Theron. Summer knew that it would likely get worse in the weeks to come, that hurt and pain, if he didn't return to her as she'd hoped. But for the moment she focused on the plan. Even if his voice whispered in her ear.

Plans are not wants. What do you want?

Summer wanted him. She wanted this. She wanted the future that she could see just beyond her reach. And with a hand around the curve of her bump, she wondered if she had the faith to make something magical happen.

CHAPTER TEN

FOUR HOURS LATER and the world looked impossibly different. Summer's head was spinning at the shocking plans she had put into motion. Her sisters looked at her, eyes wide, round but utterly thrilled.

'Are you sure you want to do this?'

Summer was so tempted to shake her head. She was terrified but also excited, as if she were on a roller coaster and never wanted to get off. So she nodded, quickly and surely. 'Yes. I am.'

'You're crazy,' Skye whispered in awe. 'But I love it.'

'Good. Because I'm going to need Benoit's help. And lots of it!'

'Duratra has incredible metalworkers. They made the necklace. I'm sure that they could help too.'

'I would *love* that, Star. I think Catherine would have too,' Summer said, the press of tears, happy ones for now, against the backs of her eyes.

They were in the office where Skye, Star and Summer's journey had started just under two months ago. Of all the rooms and corridors Summer had searched, she'd never come back to this one, knowing that the hard-faced portrait of Elias Soames sent shivers down her spine every time she caught sight of it. But somehow, at that moment, it felt poignant, *right*, that they had come full circle to end where it had all begun.

Summer sat between her sisters as Mr Beamish imperiously scrawled on the paperwork—a witness following his every signature—seemingly thankful that the whole sorry mess of the Elias Soames estate was soon to be behind him. Star peered over her shoulder at the room off to the side, where Mariam Soames and Kyros Agyros had been sequestered for the last hour.

'Do you think they're okay?' Star asked.

'He's very handsome, your father,' Skye said with a smile.

'They have a *lot* of catching up to do,' Summer said, her heart warming.

'Did you see the way she looked at him?' Skye asked. *Fireworks*, she mouthed and Star let out a snort.

'Even though it's Mum, that's still a bit—'

The door to the room opened and all three sisters squeaked and turned away as if naughty schoolgirls being caught out. Mariam Soames was blushing like one herself, and the twinkle in Kyros's eyes was something magical to Summer.

'And that concludes our business, I believe,' Mr Beamish announced, calling their attention back to him. 'The estate, the entail, all yours now that you've found the Soames diamonds.' Summer felt a sigh of relief, no longer expecting someone to magically appear and snatch it all away from them. 'Congratulations. I hope that—' he broke off, looking around at the dark, damaged house with barely concealed disgust '—you are happy here.'

The girls couldn't help but laugh as he hightailed it out of the estate with his assistant and the witness as quickly as humanly possible.

'And you are sure that this is something you want to do?' Kyros asked his daughter, everyone seeming to hold their breath.

'Absolutely,' Summer replied resolutely. 'I—*we*—couldn't be doing this without you, though. And we can't thank you enough.' Her sisters' agreement rose in the air, but Kyros seemed to shake them off, the swift jerk of his head reminding her bruised heart of Theron.

Mariam Soames looked to Kyros. 'But after Althaia…'

Summer could sense it—her mother's sadness, guilt even, about Kyros caring for another sick lover.

'It is the least I can do,' Kyros said, taking her hand in his and gazing into her eyes, 'and the least I want to do. The treatment will start the day after tomorrow and I will be there with you every second of it. And when you beat it, you will come with me to Greece and recuperate in the sun, on my island.'

Star's eyes bugged out. 'He owns an island?' she whispered, and Summer smiled.

'You own a country,' Skye chided.

'Well, not *own* and not *yet*,' she replied, fanning herself as if the thought was suddenly quite overwhelming.

'And I own an estate,' Summer said in wonder as her sisters looked at her with joy and excitement for her.

'Yeah, you do,' Skye said, gently bumping her shoulder against Summer's shoulder.

It unfurled within her, this sense of rightness and excitement. She would restore the building using the latest and safest technologies and ensure that Catherine's heritage, *their* heritage, would stand for a very, very long time.

Once again, she could have sworn she heard the sound of a child's laughter disappearing into the estate, and, whether it was prescient of the future or an echo of the past, Summer felt comforted by it. A gift, given to her by her ancestors.

The sound of wheels on gravel drew the group's attention to the windows.

'I'd hoped Beamish had left,' Skye said, failing to suppress the shiver of dislike that ran through her body.

'He must have forgotten something,' Summer said, standing from her seat.

'I'll go,' Star offered.

'That's okay,' Summer said, stretching out the slight ache across her shoulders. 'I'm sure I'll only be a moment.' She left the room before there could be any more protests. It was a strange feeling, but after weeks on her own in the estate, with her parents and her sisters here it suddenly felt crowded, a little claustrophobic even. A part of her wanted to be alone, to feel all the things that had happened to her in the last twenty-four hours. If she thought about it too hard her head started to spin.

The sound of the car grew closer and closer as she reached the front of the house and she pulled open the door in time to see a black behemoth pull to a stop. It looked like something from the army.

She frowned, a little worried now, as the passenger door opened and she heard the tail-end of an argument in heavily accented English, 'At least it's better than a convertible!'

The slam of the door drew her attention to the tall form stepping down from the beast of a car, long legs easily reaching the distance to the ground and turning on the gravel. From the handmade shoes to the expensive superfine wool trousers moulding powerful thighs, the leather belt at lean hips she had clung to, the broad expanse of chest that made her pulse trip, she knew every inch of the father of her child and would never tire of seeing him, even if he had shattered her heart.

The sensuality of his lips was inflamed by the determined slant to them, the flare in his gaze as he drew to a sudden halt, seeing her standing in the doorway at the top of the stone steps. For moments they just stood and stared, as if gorging on the sight of each other.

They both moved at the same time, starting towards each other and stopping again.

'*Gia ónoma tou Theó...*' Summer shot a glance over Theron's shoulder to see Lykos Livas standing against the monstrous vehicle with his arms crossed over his chest and an almost childlike look of irritation on his features. Summer had to suppress a smile, guessing at the translation from the obvious impatience in Lykos's voice.

Then she saw him flinch as Lykos looked over her shoulder, and she turned to find her father and mother standing behind her with her sisters off to the side. Lykos and Kyros stared each other down, before Lykos purposely cut his gaze away.

Summer frowned, wondering what had happened there but knowing that was a story for another time. Paying no more attention to them, her gaze hungrily returned to Theron. Hope bloomed in her heart and she gazed into his eyes, knowing that something was different. She'd been waiting for the shutters to come down to mask his feelings, but they didn't and she began to believe that they might never come down again.

He opened his mouth as if to speak, then stopped. She moved a step forward as he did and then stopped again.

'I love you,' he said, and her legs trembled. 'There are things I was supposed to say. A *plan*. But… I love you.'

She couldn't help but laugh gently as she repeated the words he'd once said. 'Plans are not wants.'

'I *want* you,' he said helplessly. 'With every single fibre of my being. I want you. I always have. You need to know that. But now, and for ever, I want to *be* with you. To hear you laugh, to help you cry, to be the vent for your anger, your frustration. I want to argue with you, I want to make up with you, I want to care for you, protect you, grow old with you. I just… I want to love you and be loved by you. Any plan, now or in the future, will always be for you and our child. Whether I'm with you in the same room, house or even country. Whether—' he paused, as if swallowing some deep emotion '—you want me or not.'

Her love-filled gaze cleared enough to see his sincerity, but his words brought back the memories of their argument and, despite the joy she felt at his declaration… it wasn't enough. She needed it and their child needed it. 'What changed?' she asked, shrugging helplessly.

Theron stood to his full height, never once taking his eyes from her, drawing strength from the earth beneath him to say what he needed to say, desperately hoping that Summer would know the truth of his words.

'I left because I was scared,' he said, his throat thick with emotion, the shame and hurt filling his chest. 'You asked me to be there for our child,' he said, stopping himself from explaining why. He cast a glance to where Kyros stood beside an older version of Summer and two younger women who could only be her sisters. He refused to shame either Mariam or Kyros for their choices, but he knew Summer would know the depth of her request. 'And I…that terrified me. You were right.' He shook his head, hating the way his heart trembled in his chest. 'I've lost so much family. My parents, my brother,' he said, casting a look back to Lykos, who raised a wry eyebrow. Smiling slightly, Theron realised that Lykos would always be his family. He knew the hand that Lykos had played in this, in leading him to Summer, guiding him back to where he needed to be.

He took a breath and thought of the other person he had loved and lost. 'Althaia,' he said, unable to meet Kyros's gaze. 'The thought of losing you, the thought of anything happening to you or our child… I couldn't bear it. I still can't. But even just a night without you was more painful than anything I've experienced,' he pressed on truthfully. 'And if there's even a chance that you'd consider letting me prove to you how much I love you, then please tell me. Give me hope.'

The sheen in her eyes told him there might be, but he would settle for nothing less than her words. Her heart. Even if it took him a lifetime. Behind him Lykos cleared his throat and he suddenly remembered.

'No matter what happens, though, I want you to know that the estate is yours.' He watched as her brow furrowed in confusion and he silently cursed himself. He was messing this up. 'I've spoken to Lykos and I will buy the estate.'

She stared at him, her thoughts hidden from him. 'It's not for sale,' she said quietly.

'What? You didn't find the jewels?' he demanded, shocked, a thousand fears going through his mind at once.

'We did,' Summer said, her head tilted to the side, a smile pulling at her lips. He was distracted for just a second until her words penetrated.

'But your mother's treatment?'

'I am handling that,' Kyros announced from the steps behind Summer, his arm around the woman

who Summer resembled so very much. When Theron
looked at Kyros this time, there wasn't disappointment
or rejection, there was pride, love and a determined
glint that warned Theron not to mess this up. He felt it.
A blessing. One that he would never take for granted.
He turned back to Summer, trying to read her gaze.

'So you're keeping the estate?' Theron asked, instinctively knowing how much she would like that.

'I still want a castle!' Lykos groused in the background, pulling smiles from both Theron and Summer
almost against their will.

Summer nodded. 'Benoit and Skye will help with
the redesign and Star and Khalif will arrange for help
from Duratra on the large amount of metalwork I'd
like done. I want to put my studies to use on the renovations.'

There was more to it, Theron knew. He could see it
burning in her gaze. 'You have a plan,' he said, knowing instinctively that it would be marvellous.

'But I also have a want,' she whispered, stepping
closer to him, a spark of something deliciously wicked
in her eyes.

A tendril of hope unfurled in his heart and heat
soaked into his bones. 'Tell me,' he demanded.

'I want you to ask me to marry you,' she said, closing the distance between them to inches.

He searched her gaze, the sparkle in her eyes, the
mischief, the promise.

And his heart crashed.

He pressed his forehead against hers as an ache of
sad frustration coursed through his body. 'I don't have

a ring. We left London at six-thirty in the morning. I…' he bit back a curse '…I want to do it properly. I want to give you everything you deserve,' he said, his voice rough with emotion.

She bent her head back, her hazel eyes sparkling with gold. 'Is that all?' she said with a smile, though what she could possibly find to smile about he had no idea. Until she looked back to her sisters, the taller one he imagined was Skye, who smiled broadly and threw something small towards Summer, who caught it and presented it to him.

'It's perhaps a bit unorthodox, but I think Catherine would approve,' Summer said, passing him the small ring-shaped box.

'The Soames diamonds?' he asked, and she nodded, her eyes and heart seeming as full as his own felt.

He took the velvet box, warm from her touch, in his palm and pressed it against his heart. But he wanted one last thing. He would propose no matter what, but this felt right. Felt just.

He looked up to where Summer's family had gathered by the front door of the estate, catching Kyros's eye first, then Mariam's.

'Ms Soames, Kyros, I would very much like to ask for your daughter's hand in marriage. I want you to know that I will protect her and our child unconditionally, I will love her and our child unconditionally, and I will—'

'We get the idea, Theron,' Lykos said, rolling his hand as if to say get on with it. The smaller sister with red hair hid a laugh behind her hand and the older one bit her lip as if to stop herself from smiling. The love and happiness shining from Mariam was one of the purest things Theron had ever seen. She looked up to Kyros and back to him and nodded.

'You have my blessing, *yié mou*,' Kyros said, the words *my son* miraculous to hear after all these years.

And then absolutely nothing could have pulled him away from Summer.

He took her hand in his and slowly bent to one knee, unfeeling of the bite of gravel through his trousers. Wonder and awe coursed through his body as he looked up at the woman who made him feel complete. Whole. The woman he would spend the rest of his life loving to distraction.

And there, surrounded by people bonded by blood or by choice, he knew *this* was his family: Summer and their child and the people who loved and cared for them, all brought together by Catherine and the Soames diamonds. Wetness pressed against his eyes as he looked up at the love of his life. 'Would you, Summer Soames, do me the greatest honour and be my wife, my confidante, my love, my family, my *home*?'

'Yes,' Summer said as tears rolled down her cheeks and her sisters screamed and yelled, and even Lykos seemed to clear his throat of emotion. 'Yes, I will,' she said, pulling him up from the ground and bringing him into a kiss that branded his soul as hers.

'I love you,' she whispered between presses of her lips. 'I will always love you,' she promised and Theron knew that, no matter what happened in the future, the love that he felt in that moment would fuel the rest of their lives.

EPILOGUE

Five years later...

SUMMER WAS JUST finishing her journal entry. She'd been hurrying to get it done in time, looking as the clock ticked down the minutes until—

'Mummy! Mummy? Where are you?'

Right on time, she heard Katy's not so dulcet tones calling for her, even as a smile full of love pulled at her mouth. Theron always tried to keep their mischievous daughter occupied in the kitchen for at least half an hour after dinner so that Summer could have this time, knowing how important her journalling was to her.

Quickly she put down the journal, turned off the light, closed the door to the secret room, slipped through the passageway and back into the master bedroom just before Katy burst into the room.

'Mummy, where are—' Katy descended into a fit of giggles as she realised she'd been shouting when Summer was standing right there.

'Mummy, that's naughty,' she accused. It was Summer's daughter's latest delight. Although Catherine was the name on their daughter's birth certificate, they had called her Katy from day one.

'What's naughty, sweetpea?' she asked.

'*You* are!'

'*I* am? *I* am?' Summer demanded, all mock outrage as she chased her daughter with tickle fingers and they both ended up in a hysterical heap on the bed. She didn't think that there was anything more pure, more beautiful than the sound of her daughter, out of breath from laughter.

Summer pushed a dark curl from her daughter's forehead, so happy that she had her father's deep dark eyes. But the sparkle? That was *all* Soames.

'Where are my girls?' Theron's voice boomed into the room.

'Here, Daddy. Mummy's being naughty again,' Katy said, bursting into laughter as Summer's quick tickles found her.

'Oh, really?' Theron demanded as he came into the room, staring down at them with a glint in his eye that Katy was thankfully far too young to recognise. He smiled and Summer felt it in her heart.

Summer didn't know how, but he was able to do this thing where he'd look at her and time would just *stop*. She'd feel an infinity of love in an instant and knew that she could never want for anything more.

He sighed, before checking his watch, as if he'd felt it too. His eyes widened and then he pulled a grimace. 'Katy, we have to get dressed. The others are going to be here in twenty minutes.'

Katy scrabbled up on the bed and started jumping up and down, crying, 'The others are coming!'

Even as Summer put her hand out, just in case, Theron was by the bed in an instant, plucking his daughter from the air mid-jump.

'Come on, my love. You have your new dress to—'

The scream of delight from their daughter was so loud it could have burst his eardrums but he didn't flinch, didn't loosen his hold even for a second. Cradling her to him, Theron bent over the bed, Katy now giggling at being horizontal, and kissed Summer quickly but lovingly and took their daughter off to get ready for the day.

Summer watched them go until she checked the time and jumped off the bed and threw herself into the shower. Fifteen minutes later, she was showered, dry and opening the wardrobe door, marvelling at the array of colour that was on display. She passed the teals, the beautiful bright yellows and the verdant greens. There was only one colour to be worn today.

As she came down the stairs, the beautiful scarlet silk swirled around her calves, matching the red stilettos she knew that her husband would appreciate, even if she didn't last the *full* day in them. Her fingers tripped over the red velvet ribbon Katy had insisted should wrap around the banister, and the scent of pine trees and spiced orange rose up from the lower floor. Everywhere she looked was sparkles of tinsel, rich green foliage and deep red velvet. Theron, apparently, loved Christmas as much as their daughter.

An impossibly tall spruce stood proudly in the hallway to greet every member of the family as they arrived. Giant red bows, little silver bows and American candy canes hung from the boughs while sparkling cream lights twinkled between the fronds. There was a giant silver urn on the side table with mulled wine and glasses ready for their guests.

Summer inhaled deeply and rolled her shoulders free of any stiffness, relishing the excitement and anticipation of the day ahead. In the last few years it had become her favourite part of the year because it was the one time that everyone was guaranteed to gather together. At any other point, they were spread as far and wide as Greece, Duratra, France, Costa Rica and wherever else Skye could entice Benoit to wander.

But everyone came home for Christmas.

Although Kyros hadn't been happy about it, Summer and Theron had waited until Katy was three years old before marrying. By that point, Skye had married Benoit exactly a year on from his proposal in a gorgeous outdoor wedding in France, the Soames diamond necklace as her something old. And no one had minded one bit when little Katy had burst into beautiful laughter as the priest had asked for anyone to 'speak now or forever hold your peace'.

Star had married Khalif in a stunning ceremony in Duratra's capital, where the celebrations had lasted for days and Katy had been treated like a little princess and loved every minute of it. Star had worn the Soames diadem and the interlocked necklace in honour of both Catherine and Hâtem. The joining of the two families felt fated.

But Summer's wedding to Theron had been a little closer to home.

Two years ago today, Summer had walked down these very same stairs in a wedding dress of oyster-coloured silk. The design had been similar to that of the yellow dress she had bought all those years ago in Athens. And although everyone proclaimed her to be the most beautiful bride they'd ever seen, she only had eyes for Theron.

In front of their families, those of blood and those of friendship, Summer had sworn to love her husband for eternity and a day and Theron had promised to be by her side and never leave. The glint in his eye as he'd finally made the promise that had terrified him so much was more than Summer could have ever asked for.

In a mixture of Greek and English, wreaths and rings, their love had been celebrated and cemented in the estate in Norfolk that had been in her family for hundreds of years, and Summer couldn't shake the feeling that Catherine had been watching over them that day.

Before she could round the corner, Theron appeared at the bottom of the stairs and Summer couldn't help the burst of arousal from deep within her at the sight of her husband dressed in a suit that fitted him to perfection.

As if he were feeling the same way, his eyes flashed for just a moment before he blinked. But while the intensity in his gaze had been banked, in the last five years and all their years to come his thoughts and feelings were never hidden from her again.

To her surprise, he bent to one knee.

'What are you doing?'

'Asking you to marry me.'

'But—' she broke off to laugh '—we're already married,' she said as she drew closer and closer to him.

'I know. I just want to be able to promise you that I'll never leave your side in front of our family and friends as many times as possible.'

'We don't need a lavish ceremony just for that.'

'*Just* for that?' he demanded in the same way he'd once demanded what 'just a kiss' was supposed to mean. 'If I want, I will have a hundred ceremonies to tell you how much I love you and to make unending promises to the most beautiful wife a man has ever had.'

'Theron, don't let Lykos hear you say that, or he'll be offering a *thousand* ceremonies to his wife.'

Theron laughed, standing to his full height. 'I still can't quite believe that he actually ended up with a castle,' he said, fitting her to his side and placing his hand between her shoulder blades as he liked to do. He guided her to a stop and took her hand in his, pulling her round to face him.

He slowly inched forward, his lips hovering a hair's breadth from hers, pleasure and anticipation rising within her as she held onto the tease, waiting to see which one of them broke first this time.

The moment was broken by the peal of the doorbell.

Theron smiled and whispered, 'You owe me a

kiss,' into her ear before he turned and braced himself against the screams of her sisters and nieces as they rushed the couple with hugs, laughter and love. Through the chaos Summer saw Benoit following through the entrance, talking to Khalif about the incredible memorial project for his brother and sister-in-law and she couldn't help the tendril of professional curiosity getting the better of her. Theron caught her eye and understood her desire, enticing her sisters and nieces away to meet Katy, so that she could catch up on how the bridge and conservation area between two kingdoms in the Middle East was coming along.

Before long, Katy came running to find her and pull her back to the living room, where piles and piles of presents were being unloaded to her mounting horror.

'I thought we said only one present each,' Summer said, feeling a little worried.

Star laughed gently. 'We did. And we stuck to it. But we wanted to take some gifts to the children's ward at Norfolk and Norwich Hospital. The boys are going to take the girls there this afternoon.'

Understanding dawned in her eyes and she nodded, feeling a spread of love for the generosity they were able to share, but also the tug of a promise they had made when Mariam had first started her treatment.

Five years on and Mariam had received the all-clear and was officially cancer-free. The celebration planned for that evening, after Mariam and Kyros flew in from Greece, would be incredible. But no less important than the personal moment the sisters had planned for that afternoon.

Over a leisurely late brunch, that Skye argued with Theron was more lunch, and Lykos, who had arrived with his wife, rolled his eyes and complained about, saying the English didn't know anything about food, which Theron wholly agreed with, Summer felt love for her family rise up around her and fill the house completely.

In her wildest dreams she couldn't have imagined such a future. And it was all thanks to Catherine Soames. She caught her sisters' eyes and, as if they all felt and thought the same way, they quietly excused themselves from the table. Their husbands, understanding, kept the children distracted and soon Summer heard the entire group getting into their respective cars and heading out to the hospital for the family tradition that had started the year after Skye's little girl had spent a terrifying three months in hospital over Christmas. She could see that Skye was torn, wanting to go with them, and Summer put a hand on her arm for comfort.

'It's okay,' Skye insisted. 'There will be plenty more years for that. *This* is something I want to do.'

'It's something we all want to do,' insisted Star, and Summer led them to a section of wood panelling beside the master bedroom that they hadn't seen before. 'Wait…what…?'

Summer smiled and shrugged mischievously. 'Well, we were renovating so many of the areas and I thought that just because they were secret passageways doesn't mean they have to be *grim* passageways.'

Skye's eyes grew round, staring at the panelling

and finally seeing the faint impression of a secret door. 'You didn't! Benoit didn't say anything,' she chided.

'We wanted it to be a surprise,' Summer replied.

'Naughty,' Star teased.

'You're the second person who's said that to me today,' she said, confused. 'I don't think I'm naughty at all.'

Skye made a face and Summer gently nudged her with her shoulder.

Star looked up impatiently. 'Well, what are we waiting for?'

Summer laughed. 'You.'

'Me?'

'Yes. The key.'

'But that's for the… Wait. Oh, Summer!'

She smiled as Star produced the key and found the lock on a door that looked like part of the mahogany panelling beside the master bedroom.

The key slipped in as if it had been used only the day before. Which it hadn't. Summer had a secret entrance from the master bedroom to Catherine's hidden room, but she'd wanted separate access for her sisters whenever they wanted to use it.

The door opened to a gently lit corridor, grained wooden flooring and smooth plastered walls. The corridor wrapped around the bedroom and all the way to the small room Catherine had hidden the Soames diamonds in. A room which had also undergone a bit of a transformation.

Skye and Star looked around, wide-eyed, at the little room that now contained shelves and three chairs and was cosy and beautiful.

'This room is now separate from the rest of the secret passageways,' Summer explained. 'We thought that the girls might enjoy being able to use the other passageways when we're ready to show them. The renovations have made them safe and secure and I have promised Theron a thousand times that they won't get lost in them,' she assured her sisters. 'But this room is separate and can only be accessed by us. For the moment.'

Skye and Star nodded. 'It's perfect,' they said together, each taking a seat in one of the chairs.

'Have you brought them?' Summer asked.

The girls produced little velvet boxes and placed them on the table in between them. Star had brought the diadem she had worn on her wedding day, Skye the necklace and, with a little bit of a heart-wrench, Summer twisted the beautiful engagement ring from her finger, before replacing her wedding ring.

For the last five years, Summer and her sisters had been talking about the idea of returning the Soames diamonds and Catherine's journals to the secret room that had kept them safe for so many years. Unaccountably, each of the sisters felt strongly that it was the right thing to do and had decided to leave their own journals and letters for future generations of Soames women.

For a while the sisters talked, caught up, shared the stories of their lives, laughed, cried and loved, until a text from Theron announced their return. The women placed the Soames diamonds in a box on the shelf next to Catherine's journals, and their own diaries. In the years to come, those shelves would become full with the writings from generations of Soames women, each telling their own story of adversity and triumph, loss, but most of all love.

But, for now, Skye, Star and Summer left the room, locking it behind them and returning to their families, ready and waiting for Mariam and Kyros's arrival.

Later that night, as Summer got ready for bed, Theron came out of the bathroom, a towel slung low on his hips and drying his hair with another, and she marvelled at just how handsome her husband was. Not once had their attraction dimmed, even through their occasional arguments and their even more occasional hurts, and Summer wanted her husband with the same ferocity as she had on the beach at Piraeus that first time.

Theron's gaze flickered from her eyes to her ring finger and back again.

'I'm sorry, I should have said—'

He smiled, knowing and loving, the look in his eyes cutting her off mid-sentence. 'You didn't need to, *agápi mou*,' he said, kneeling on the bed, tossing the towel back into the bathroom and reaching into the drawer of his bedside table. He produced a small white box she'd not seen before. 'I know. I see you. And I love you. More than anything in the world, Summer Soames. I am the proudest man alive that you chose me and I will spend every day being worthy of it.'

Love bloomed in Summer's heart, strong, powerful, fierce and determined. He opened the box to reveal a stunning diamond engagement ring. It was different to the Soames diamond she had worn, but it was just as special to Summer.

Before reaching for it, she placed her hand on her husband's. 'Five years ago I went to Greece, looking for a part of me that I knew was missing. A part that had felt missing my entire life. And there, in Athens, I found it. Not Kyros, not my father. But you, Theron Thiakos. You are the other half of me and you will always have me and my heart, in yours.'

That night they made love until the sun crested on the horizon and not one of their family minded that they missed breakfast. Apart from Lykos, who grumbled about it for the rest of the day.

* * * * *

WE HOPE YOU ENJOYED
THIS BOOK FROM

H HARLEQUIN

PRESENTS

Escape to exotic locations where passion knows no bounds.

Welcome to the glamorous lives of royals and billionaires, where passion knows no bounds. Be swept into a world of luxury, wealth and exotic locations.

8 NEW BOOKS AVAILABLE EVERY MONTH!

#3969 CINDERELLA'S BABY CONFESSION
by Julia James

Alys's unexpected letter confessing to the consequences of their one unforgettable night has ironhearted Nikos reconsidering his priorities. He'll bring Alys to his Greek villa, where he *will* claim his heir. By first unraveling the truth...and then her!

#3970 PREGNANT BY THE WRONG PRINCE
Pregnant Princesses
by Jackie Ashenden

Molded to be the perfect queen, Lia's sole rebellion was her night in Prince Rafael's powerful arms. She never dared dream of more. But now Rafael's stopping her arranged wedding—to claim her and the secret she carries!

#3971 STRANDED WITH HER GREEK HUSBAND
by Michelle Smart

Marooned on a Greek island with her estranged but gloriously attractive husband, Keren has nowhere to run. Not just from the tragedy that broke her and Yannis apart, but from the joy and passion she's tried—and failed—to forget...

#3972 RETURNING FOR HIS UNKNOWN SON
by Tara Pammi

Eight years after a plane crash left Christian with no memory of his convenient vows to Priya, he returns—and learns of his heir! To claim his family, he makes Priya an electrifying proposal: three months of living together...as man and wife.

#3973 ONE SNOWBOUND NEW YEAR'S NIGHT
by Dani Collins

Rebecca has one New Year's resolution: divorce Donovan Scott. Being snowbound at his mountain mansion isn't part of the plan. And what happens when it becomes clear the chemistry that led to their elopement is still very much alive?

#3974 VOWS ON THE VIRGIN'S TERMS
The Cinderella Sisters
by Clare Connelly

A four-week paper marriage to Luca to save her family from destitution seems like an impossible ask for innocent Olivia... Until he says yes! And then, on their honeymoon, the most challenging thing becomes resisting her irresistible new husband...

#3975 THE ITALIAN'S BARGAIN FOR HIS BRIDE
by Chantelle Shaw

By marrying heiress Paloma, self-made tycoon Daniele will help her protect her inheritance. In return, he'll gain the social standing he needs. Their vows are for show. The heat between them is definitely, maddeningly, *not*!

#3976 THE RULES OF THEIR RED-HOT REUNION
by Joss Wood

When Aisha married Pasco, she naively followed her heart. Not anymore! Back in the South African billionaire's world—as his business partner—she'll rewrite the terms of their relationship. Only, their reunion takes a dangerously scorching turn...

Van slid the door open and stepped inside only to have Becca
squeak and dance her feet, nearly dropping the groceries she'd
picked up.

"You knew I was here," he insisted. "That's why I woke you, so
you would know I was here and you wouldn't do that. I *live* here,"
he said for the millionth time, because she'd always been leaping
and screaming when he came around a corner.

"Did you? I never noticed," she grumbled, setting the bag on the
island and taking out the milk to put it in the fridge. "I was alone
here so often, I forgot I was married."

"*I* noticed that," he shot back with equal sarcasm.

They glared at each other. The civility they'd conjured in
those first minutes upstairs was completely abandoned—probably
because the sexual awareness they'd reawakened was still hissing
and weaving like a basket of cobras between them, threatening to
strike again.

Becca looked away first, thrusting the eggs into the fridge along
with the pair of rib eye steaks and the package of bacon.

She hated to be called cute and hated to be ogled, so Van tried
not to do either, but *come on*. She was curvy and sleepy and wearing
that cashmere like a second skin. She was shorter than average and
had always exercised in a very haphazard fashion, but nature had
gifted her with a delightfully feminine figure-eight symmetry. Her

ample breasts were high and firm over a narrow waist, then her hips flared into a gorgeous, equally firm and round ass. Her fine hair was a warm brown with sun-kissed tints, her mouth wide, and her dark brown eyes positively soulful.

When she smiled, she had a pair of dimples that he suddenly realized he hadn't seen in far too long.

"I don't have to be here right now," she said, slipping the coffee into the cupboard. "If you're going skiing tomorrow, I can come back while you're out."

"We're ringing in the New Year right here." He chucked his chin at the windows that climbed all the way to the peak of the vaulted ceiling. Beyond the glass, the frozen lake was impossible to see through the thick and steady flakes. A gray-blue dusk was closing in.

"You have four-wheel drive, don't you?" Her hair bobbled in its knot, starting to fall as she snapped her head around. She fixed her hair as she looked back at him, arms moving with the mysterious grace of a spider spinning her web. "How did you get here?"

"Weather reports don't apply to me," he replied with self-deprecation. "Gravity got me down the driveway and I won't get back up until I can start the quad and attach the plow blade." He scratched beneath his chin, noted her betrayed glare at the windows.

Believe me, sweetheart. I'm not any happier than you are.

He thought it, but immediately wondered if he was being completely honest with himself.

"How was the road?" She fetched her phone from her purse, distracting him as she sashayed back from where it hung under her coat. "I caught a rideshare to the top of the driveway and walked down. I can meet one at the top to get back to my hotel."

"Plows will be busy doing the main roads. And it's New Year's Eve," he reminded her.

"So what am I supposed to do? Stay here? All night? With *you*?"

"Happy New Year," he said with a mocking smile.

Don't miss
One Snowbound New Year's Night.
Available January 2022 wherever
Harlequin Presents books and ebooks are sold.

Harlequin.com